# Carve your own path to success

*Perspectives of managing growth
in dynamic Environments*

# Carve your own path to success

*Perspectives of managing growth
in dynamic Environments*

**Alan Doulton**

**Lithouse
2019**

Carve your own path to success: *Perspectives of managing growth in dynamic Environments* — published by Lithouse, Delhi.

© Author, 2019

ISBN: 978-93-88945-34-9

*Laser typeset by Lithouse, Delhi.*

# Contents

# Contents

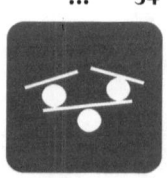

# Acknowledgment

The knowledge acquisition of this magnitude would not have been possible without the support of many executives on the ground at all levels as well as scholars and other practitioners. They shared their insights and allowed me to explore their operations. I thank them.

I also thank the numerous persons that helped in editing the book. Besides editing they provided a range of perspectives to make this book more meaningful for the reader.

This book would not have been possible without the constant support, encouragement and constructive feedback from the late R. V Krishnan (Chairman BDB India Pvt Ltd.), Nikhil Kapadia (Deutsche Bank) Brig. Sharad Luktuke (Indian Army), Nash and Hooty Hansotia (Primerica) and Andrew Pinto (Executive Mentor). I owe them my gratitude.

I must specially mention my golf buddies who provided ground reality and hard business-truth insights on and off the course. Many thanks to them.

This whole effort has been possible only because of the support of my family Yvonne, Melanie and Mark. I give them my heartfelt thanks.

Dear Readers

It is good to know that you are interested in exploring the possibilities of achieving your full potential through thought triggers presented in 'Carve your own path to success'.

The learnings from working in five different companies for 25 years and from running my own consulting firm, Alan Associates, for another 25 years, is shared in this book. The mission of Alan Associates was to provide, individuals and organizations with professional assistance in solving problems to achieve their goals. The services included consulting, mentoring and training interventions at various hierarchical levels along tactical and strategic lines.

The five companies I worked for were in different industry sectors. During the consulting period I had the privilege to formally mentor and coach over 500 'C' level executives besides conducting issue-based training for about 5000 middle and senior level managers and about 12,000 junior executives. During my engagements with several companies over the past 50 years, I have had the privilege to interact with executives at different levels. Some of the companies or their subsidiaries across the globe were: 3DGS (Dassault India), Areva, Atlas Copco, Alstom, Amphenol, Bajaj Tempo, Bank of India Cap Gemini, Cognizant Technology Solutions, Eaton, Faurecia, Hindustan Aeronautics Ltd., Honeywell, HSBC, Human Factors International, IBM, Infosys, Kanoo Group, KPIT, Larsen & Toubro, MICO (Bosch India), Persistent Systems, Primerica, QNB (Qatar), Tata

Consultancy Services, WIPRO. These executives of different nationalities came from multinational, transnational, private, public and government organizations. My experience together with research and experimentation has given me the confidence to share my thoughts on how to carve your own path to success.

This book is meant to help you reflect on where you are, how you can excel in the current scenario and what you want to achieve.

It is meant for top performers at senior levels. It is therefore not intended to be a onetime or easy read. You may like to consider it a side table guide for continuous and easy reference. This is because your reflection will always be governed by parameters impacting current scenarios. Constant change requires new paths to success. As outlined in the book: You can be good when following proven track records but to be great you need to 'Carve your own path to success'.

Finally, I would like to remind you that the book may provide you knowledge and even trigger your wisdom but results will only come from action. Hence implementation is the key to success, knowledge and wisdom will only help.

Alan Doulton

# Reviews

Alan Doulton has distilled 50 years of his wide experience in the corporate world into a book that tells you how to build a successful career. It provides helpful advice and guidance to young professionals, illustrated through numerous case studies. The middle manager will find the book useful in working out plans for further progress and for senior managers the case studies provide useful parallels and perspectives to help understand corporate strategy. Strongly recommended.

*Mathai Joseph*
Formerly Executive Director,
Tata Research Design and Development Centre

Alan Doulton has shared his knowledge and insight gained through experience over several years for the benefit of aspiring leaders. He highlights the importance of connectivity in building successful careers and brings out interesting concepts aptly through his case studies in the book. This greatly enhances the value of understanding. In a cluttered marketplace of leadership writings, this book stands out and is a must read for all who wish to progress and achieve success right through their careers.

*S. A. Bhat*
Former Chairman and Managing Director
Indian Overseas Bank

Carve Your Own Path to Success' addresses the very real and intimate problem of 'Teaching an old dog new tricks'. Alan has highlighted the problem of resting on one's laurels through comprehensive and apt examples in case studies. The most interesting aspect brought out in the book is on how to manage intangibles like managing grey areas or inter departmental conflicts or how to prevent a 'silo' attitude from setting-in within an organization. This book is applicable for both profit and non-profit organizations including monoliths like the Armed Forces. I feel it is a must read for senior leadership and aspirants to high places.

*Pradeep V Naik*
Air Chief Marshal (Retired),
Former Chief of Air Staff – Indian Air Force

'Carve your own path to success' is full of practical and descriptive case studies from a spectrum of public and private sector industries, inclusive of government and military. Alan has leveraged his experience in observing the behavior of people in leadership. This book which is grounded and easy to connect with is recommended for middle and top leaders who wish to go beyond abstract concepts and are interested in a concrete approach to decision making. Those who are striving to take control of their own destiny.

*Raymond Noronha*
Lt General (Retired),
Former Corps Commander - Indian Army

"I think Alan Doulton's book is required reading for aspiring and upwardly mobile executives. It's a compelling read with many pragmatic suggestions. I was particularly pleased at the focus on the "human element" and the personal growth potential aspects. His comments on personal networking are also extremely relevant and appropriate.

*John R Wright*
Former Chief Executive of Clydesdale & Yorkshire Banks

This book represents the author's work experience over 50 years in business and industry fortified with mentoring and coaching of over 500 senior business professionals to carve and reach the path to success. This is a rich monograph that goes beyond any textbook or google search and unfolds the unique corporate success experience of the author that compels the reader to venture into similar paths for success.

*Fr. Ozzie Mascarenhas, SJ*
JRD TATA Chair Professor of Business Ethics,
XLRI Jamshedpur, India

# Prologue

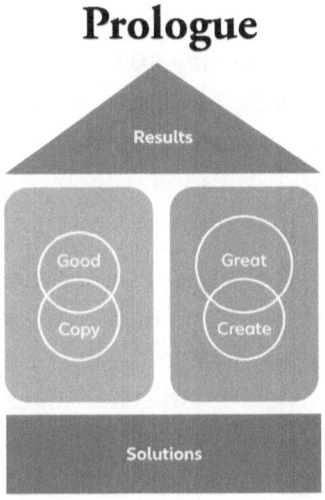

**Copy to be Good - Create to be Great**

Through most of my work life I kept thinking of what makes certain professionals more successful than others and though I discussed my thoughts with many people and went through quite a few research papers, books and articles I was not very satisfied with what I learnt.

During my work experience of over 50 years in both business and industry, I have mentored and coached over 500 senior professionals and business people in navigating their paths to growth successfully. In helping them carve their paths to success, I uncovered several diverse and complex issues that impact personal growth and must be managed to achieve any degree of success. These issues cover a variety of situations across a range of business functions. In this book, I present ideas and case studies to give different and varied perspectives on how handling of situations has led to success or failure.

The idea for this book started from a casual conversation with a director who was managing a major country specific business line for one of the top 10 financial institutions in the world. He was growing the business at 40% and was considered one of the best in the industry at that point of time. I learnt that he was very good at his job without any formal personal development for the past 10 years.

Surprised at this, I reviewed his work style and found it was mostly transactional. In this context my assessment was that he was not equipped to move to the next level or if he did, he would not be very successful. I therefore suggested that he attend a senior executive program. A month later he attended a 3-week top management program at a leading business college in London.

On his return, I asked how he had benefited from the program. After some discussion I realized that the management concepts shared during the program did not significantly impact his knowledge level. The learning mostly came through his interaction with the 25 other directors who were participants in the program. The case studies discussed during the program provided insights as to how his peers would think through issues and act in those situations. This was the learning; the subject matter was just used to facilitate the sharing of thought processes.

Having understood this, I began to appreciate that personal development for senior executives takes place by sharing experiences amongst their peers. This development is further enhanced by collaboratively exploring innovative solutions to a variety of situations.

The central theme of this 'Case Study' centric book is to motivate self-reflection for the purpose of self-development. Each chapter contains a number of case studies for you to analyze your own responses and compare them with the perspective of others.

The aim is to help determine the best path to success by making intelligent decisions and by seizing opportunities along the journey.

But what is success? Being successful means achievement of desired visions and goals. Making the right decisions along the way helps in moving closer to your goal. There are many steps to a goal. These steps have their own achievement parameters. Hence, the journey is as important as the goal. Having said this it is crucial to remember that environments and routes to a goal most often change along the way. Sometimes the goals, which are set based on several assumptions, may change because of altered or new environmental influencing factors. In a constantly changing world, it is therefore strongly recommended to craft your own route to success in order to achieve optimum results. Following an earlier proven track in a different environment may not yield the best results. Hence the title: "Carve your own path to success"

**Planned Paths and Adopted Paths**

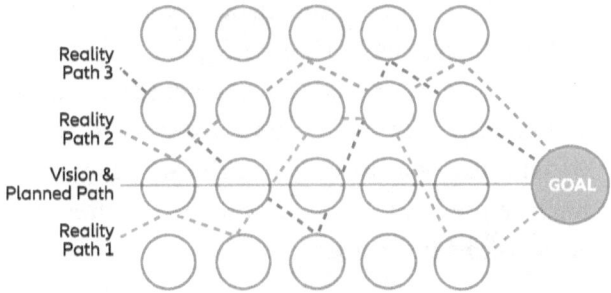

It is important to note that you do not always need to carve your own path from scratch. It means that you can often get better results by studying proven paths and then configuring your own based on the demands of the current environmental influences.

Finally, the case studies presented in this book are based on my observations and experiences. All of them have been altered to maintain confidentiality.

## Who is this book for?

This book is primarily meant for top performers at senior levels who are unaware of the nuances of their capabilities that have made them successful. These nuances go beyond the standard competency boxes used for assessment. In other words, there are intangible factors that begin to take precedence over the normal competencies that have worked at lower levels. Most HR professionals are oblivious to these facets that are the core of success at higher levels. Even world leading conglomerates do not officially consider role capability maturity factors, such as eco-system management or contribution perception management, that are essential to success. These are some of the ideas discussed in this book.

At a personal level the central theme of this book is to motivate self-reflection for the purpose of personal development. Each chapter will contain a number of case studies to support a concept. These cases may bring back personal memories or experiences you have observed. Some may appear to be from your own company, companies you have worked in or know about. This will help you to visualize the situation in a better manner, analyze the issue more accurately and prepare you to take better decisions in future.

This book may be considered as a 'thought trigger' to prompt insight into situations thereby helping to formulate better context driven solutions. Hence to manage personal growth better "Carve Your Own Path to Success" may be used as a 'thought trigger' referential guide.

Wish you a thought provoking read.

## Career Progression and Knowledge Acquisition

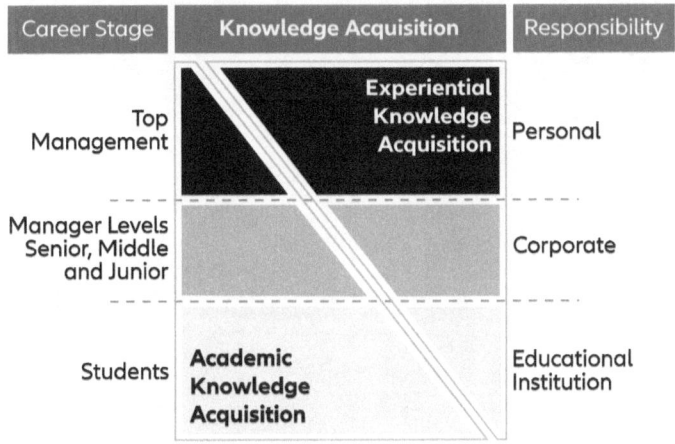

## Chapter 1

# Managing the Transition Journey

### Introduction

In life, the only constant is change. This applies to professional life as well. For every professional, role transitions take place by design or default. Being prepared to manage the transition is the key to success.

Whether an entrepreneur, a CEO, a senior professional or manager, your role can change for a variety of reasons. Whether by means of a promotion or changes in the organization (growth in business, mergers, acquisitions, restructuring), role transitions are normal and to be expected in any career path.

The old assumption is that the skills which make you successful in a particular role will help you achieve success in a new role, is a myth. Growth is based more on potential than current capabilities. To ensure a proper capability fit, people are sometimes asked to take up future roles for a probation period before being officially moved into the new position. Most people feel that their current capabilities are the reason, they are given new roles or assignments. This however is not true in most cases. It is the potential capabilities that are considered prior to selection of a candidate for a new assignment or role. 'What brought you here, won't take you there', is a phrase coined to highlight that capabilities considered predominant in one role are not necessarily the most important or relevant in a different role. Marshall Goldsmith in his book "What Got You Here Won't Get You There" has brought out this concept very well. There are numerous angles to this trend of thought. "Carve your own path to success" explores one of those angles in the chapter "Managing the Transition Journey."

Many people plateau in their positions because of this assumption and are often unable to understand why. The basic reason for this is that the type of capabilities required for a new role is based on the changed context related to the operating environments and performance requirements. For example, a Marketing or Finance VP who becomes the CEO of an organisation will need to develop or use skills other than those that brought success in earlier roles. Or, when an organisation doubles or triples its turnover, senior managers and entrepreneurs need to change their style of functioning along with their strategies and systems. That size and spread of business operations make a difference is clearly seen as companies move from operating nationally to become global players. Additionally, as you take on higher roles, your 'emotional quotient' becomes more important than your 'intelligence quotient.' This is because in higher positions you need to work with more people from different specialisations, cultures and backgrounds to get the job done.

Role transition management is a complex exercise that requires realignment of personal contributions to the job and therefore, needs to be given special consideration. Neglect in transition management could easily turn a high performing, successful executive into a mediocre one or even make him a 'failure.'

There are no rules of thumb for realignment of existing capabilities or the development of new capabilities to meet the requirements in a changed context due to role transitioning. It is an iterative process that requires continuous reading of feedback signals for course correction. Take the case of Pandesic, an Intel-SAP venture that closed down within three years in 2000 despite both companies putting their best people to manage the Joint Venture startup. (Reference: Disruptive Innovation: The Christensen Collection). The pre-transition role of these people was to manage running operations and not to manage startups, which is a completely different ball game. Realignment of their capability application priorities, or developing new capabilities to meet a startup environment was quite difficult for them. It is something like moving from a stable or fairly well-known environment to situations with a lesser degree of predictability. Stable organizations have policies, systems and processes to aid managers. In a startup however, management is more experiential and iterative in nature till systems and processes are established. This requires managers with quite a different psyche and background experience.

Role change can be for lateral as well as vertical shifts and all aspects discussed are applicable to both. However, for vertical shifts an attribute often not considered is the ability to manage grey areas and the inherent stress that is part-and-parcel of senior roles. The dictum 'the higher you go, the thicker the fog' holds true as the unknowns increase in senior positions. To restate: In junior managerial positions, you manage through POWER (instructions); at senior levels, you use PROCESSES (systems); and at top management levels, you operate on PROMISES. That is because at senior levels, commitments are often based on many assumptions and unknowns. They therefore carry much stress. Donald Sull of

London Business School has brought out the different aspects of power, processes and promises in management in his articles on "Promise Based Management – The Essence of Execution". These are in great depth and of much value. "Carve your own path to success" only emphasizes the stress aspect.

This chapter discusses role transitions to help reflect on the nuances related to career shifts or transitions which in turn could provide thought triggers in your personal context.

Schematic Diagram: Appreciating the need for reprioritization of capability application in new roles

*Summary: Role transition management is a journey that requires self-awareness to make the right changes (in terms of capability application) at the right time. The reprioritization of existing and development of additional capabilities in a new role is the key to success. It can only happen when one is able to identify and deliver through the particular key competencies required for success in the new role.*

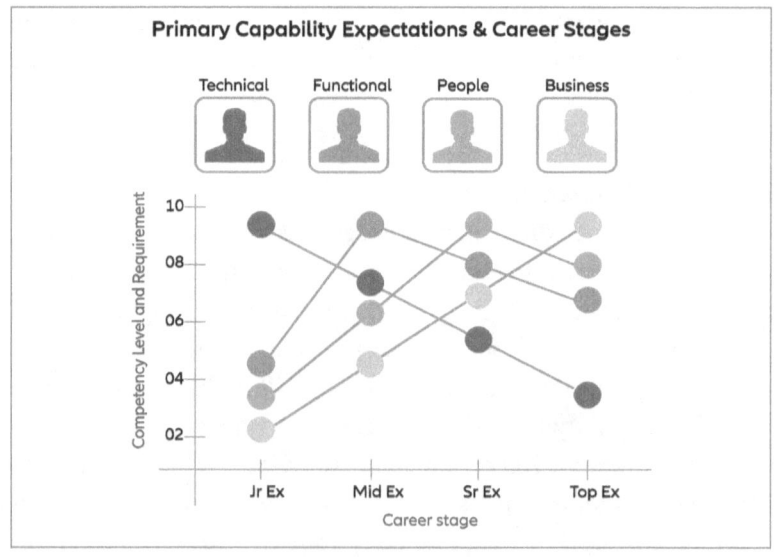

# Managing the Transition Journey

## Case Studies

### Case 1: Self-development pays off

A multinational company in the energy sector had a few business units in India. To grow its India business, it planned expansion through the acquisition of local companies. One company on its radar was a 20-year old, family-owned enterprise based in Western India. The enterprise was on the decline due to inappropriate strategies and a conservative, change-resistant management. However, as the overall financial picture showed it was actually quite stable, the bottom-line assessment by the multinational was: the price being right, the acquisition would give it a strategic geographic advantage.

Delving deeper, the enterprise systems in the family-owned firm were found to be non-existent in many areas. Many operations were person dependent and, above all, the competence of a sizeable number of employees was below average (they were retained by the owners only on account of their proven loyalty over the years). There were some very good people who showed much promise, but, as the family leadership had lost steam, they were floundering while trying to keep the company afloat.

On taking over the firm, the multinational hired a veteran Indian director and put him in charge of revitalising and aligning the firm to its standards. He knew the MNC's systems and had set up similar units in India. He also understood the psyche of the MNC's senior management, comprised of Britishers, Europeans, Americans, and one or two non-resident Indians. He was a good fit because he had both local and global knowledge and experience.

After the first two years, it was obvious the director would have to appoint a CEO for the day-to-day-running of the company. There were three key people eligible in house -- the production head, the marketing head, and the financial controller. The perception, from day one, of most local senior executives, was that either the marketing or production head would be elevated to the CEO position. The financial controller, though brilliant, did not appear to be under serious consideration for the top slot. This was because he was involved in the financial aspects of business operations only and did not have much exposure to the other business functions like marketing and production. Also, the parent company had strong financial and internal audit systems in place, which made financial reporting pretty standard and closely controlled.

However, the financial controller who was ambitious and wanted to be considered as a contender for the CEO position, was undeterred – he gauged the situation as an opportunity and started visiting the shop floor to study and understand the production process and other delivery related issues. After tackling finance-related issues like cost of work in progress and inventories, he proceeded to analyse machine set-up time vis-à-vis the manufacturing time of production cycles. This brought bottlenecks, machine capacity, and line-balancing issues to light.

On the marketing front, the proactive financial controller started reviewing outstanding collection and delivery shortage cases aggressively. Continuing his deep dive approach, he began to work with the sales team and gave them ideas on managing advance payment schedules, offering discounts, and other finance variations that would make their proposals more attractive to customers. After observing his contribution for over two years the production and marketing departments began to regularly invite him for their internal meetings.

Reviewing the financial controller's self-development strategy, it was noted he had dedicated 10-12 extra hours per week to educate himself and help others. This amounted to a laudable 1,000 extra hours over a two-and-a-half-year period. The time and effort together with his high level of business intelligence helped him learn other aspects of the business to complement his strengths in finance. This made him the obvious choice when it was finally time to select the CEO.

After five years at the helm as CEO, he was asked to take additional charge of another unit, and when he was nine years into managing two units as CEO, he was inducted to the parent company's Asia Pacific board.

> *Message: What brought you here won't take you there. Acquisition of additional competencies to meet new role requirements is important for achieving the desired success.*

## Case 2: Learn before you leap

The CEO of a large, successful information technology firm had to be replaced immediately as he was leaving the company to join a competitor. The board had to find a successor at short notice and in the process they discovered the presence of large egos and internal rivalry among the second-level managers: Those managing the various business streams were unwilling to report to any of their peers if they were selected as the next CEO. Recruiting a replacement too, however good, would cause an upset in the organisation's functioning and lead to attrition at the higher levels if the outsider did not manage the corporate dynamics well.

So, after much discussion and negotiation with over 30 top-level executives, the board chose the finance head as he had done some exceptional work to enhance the profitability of the company and was a well-respected, non-controversial figure. However, he was inexperienced, young and not a people-oriented person. In fact, he was viewed as a 'bean counter.'

In a short span of time, the newly-elevated CEO started holding reviews of the different business streams. Though he had attended a few review meetings as an invitee in the past, he was not fully conversant with the dynamic nature of such meetings. He was not only unaware of the undercurrents, but also which aspects were essential and which were okay to let go; which systems could be used to support a point and which were not to be taken seriously. He did extensive homework before conducting the review sessions. Instead of using the information gathered from his pre-review study to collaboratively work on solutions with the business and operation heads, he used it to put them on the back foot. The heads slowly started distancing themselves from the CEO.

Initially, the department heads did not take him too seriously and thought their former colleague, now appointed CEO, would let things go, but he began insisting on changing the way things were done. They felt he did not understand the business while he felt he was not being taken seriously. Consequently, he started throwing his weight around by pulling up top executives in the presence of their peers, demanding unrealistic business commitments, and taking a tough stand on slippages in areas not critical for end results.

The new CEO did not appreciate that the commitments at junior levels were based on practices or known factors that made end results highly predictable; at mid-level commitments were based on processes or programmed factors that made end results fairly predictable; and, at the topmost level commitments were educated guesses or promises based on grey area assumptions.

The previous CEO had a good idea of the thought process behind the commitments made and the executives knew this. Hence when he made statements or questioned the executives, they readily accepted his point of view and discussed alternate solutions.

Similar statements made by the new CEO were not taken with the same seriousness by the senior executives. The new CEO did not appreciate this as he did not realise that credibility and image perception impact the degree of acceptance. Being correct is not good enough.

The new incumbent's style of functioning led senior executives to play safe, withdraw or exit. In just six months of the erstwhile financial controller assuming his new position, several good managers left to join the earlier CEO or other competitors. The board started receiving feedback that not only was the top management unhappy with the new CEO, the second-level managers were unhappy too. Organisational growth, which had been on the fast track, had started slowing down.

The board thus called the CEO they had chosen and advised him to go slow. They further suggested he start restructuring the organisation by creating two new positions under him – one, of a chief operating officer (COO) to look after the operations of the company and second, of a marketing-cum-business head. This, they reckoned, would provide a layer to iron out issues between him and the functional heads, and the situation would ease. He could then begin to go a bit slow and concentrate on learning the ropes and building his credibility before taking tough stands.

By working on the board's advice the CEO learned that people have to grow into a new position -- to learn before they leap. He is now successfully managing the business and the board who could also be credited for handling the situation well, are happy with his performance.

---

*Message: Being correct in what you say is often not good enough. Your credibility and image is the key for others to accept your point of view.*

## Case 3: From a brilliant engineer to an unsuccessful CEO

An engineering conglomerate SFTI, headquartered in Europe set up an R&D subsidiary 4SSI, in India with about 50 people operating in four streams of research. As the work was very interesting and the compensation higher than that offered by some of the best manufacturing companies in the country, 4SSI was able to recruit the best talent and the unit soon grew to 600 engineers providing solutions for plants not only in Europe but around the globe.

As the experts had to travel extensively and the administrative and management work increased significantly, the parent company decided to appoint an Indian CEO to run the operations. This would allow more time for the engineers to focus on their work. It tried to hire a CEO from outside but in discussions with the unit's core team of leaders they always found the fit would not work. Finally, the SFTI management decided to select a CEO from the core team. After discussing with all the team members, they selected Rajan, a member who contributed the most and was well liked. He was a brilliant engineer with a supportive nature.

For the initial six months, all went well and everyone cooperated to help Rajan. Then, slowly, fissures appeared – initially, over small issues like travel and administration, followed by project reviews and, finally, technical domains. As Rajan had a research bent of mind, he delved deep into everything he looked at, asking questions about areas that the stream leaders did not give due importance to.

Being engineers, they felt that things like small deviations in project resources, costs and timelines were not as important as the quality and technical aspects of the solution. The SFTI management, too, was not really bothered as the benefits of low-cost R&D from India outweighed any deviations. However, Rajan, a bit of a perfectionist, sought to keep track of the deviations as he wanted to be fully aware of everything and decide how much slack he would allow. He needed to be kept informed of all situations in a timely manner so that he would be in total control of everything around him.

Soon, signs of irritation started appearing among the core members and they subtly began to act in a non-cooperative manner. They also began escalating issues to Rajan that were earlier managed quietly and successfully within their teams. This forced Rajan to shift his focus from engineering R&D towards administration. He began getting frustrated and worse still, taking out his frustrations on junior support staff and engineers. The once happy and synergised unit turned into a battlefield between the various streams and Rajan.

The SFTI management began to notice the strained relations between the core team and Rajan, but did not take it too seriously until the tense atmosphere started to manifest itself in attrition and significant cost and time over-runs. It came to the stage where they had to take a call on replacing Rajan with either someone from outside or another core team member. In replacing Rajan, they would lose a brilliant engineer who had contributed tremendously to the company in its early days. They therefore decided to help him set up a company of his own that could work in close cooperation with 4SSI. They even agreed to provide him a continuous flow of hi-tech projects in his line of specialisation over the next five years.

The decision made Rajan look good and also helped SFTI to meet its obligations through the new company. The new incumbent, Arun, a core team member was an average performer who had good management, administrative and people skills. Arun had been keenly observing the stressful situation and team dynamics within 4SSI for the past 18 months. After assessing the situation Arun decided to pace himself while getting into the new role. The SFTI management also provided him adequate support to help him gain the confidence of the rest of the team. The approach they adopted eventually worked out well for all concerned.

> *Message: Success in one role does not always guarantee success in another. Transition is not a simple and straightforward exercise. It needs to be taken seriously. An incumbent must assess the situation, inclusive of stakeholder agendas and dynamics, before getting into ground level details.*

## Case 4: 'Self Development' – A personal responsibility

A multi-level marketing company with four product streams was one of the top three in its business category. Its success largely came from recruiting agents in large numbers and training them extensively in the field. Through training sessions, they focused on sales pitches specifically tailored to motivate product purchasers to become commission agents. In this way, they could recover the spend on a product and at the same time become self-employed. This approach attracted recruits in droves, but most of them left in a short span of time as they realised that, in their enthusiasm, they had ignored most of the realities in the field. Over 90 per cent left in the first three months, and most of those that did hang on eventually left within a year, resulting in an overall attrition of about 98 per cent. Yet, it was no cause for concern as this was an accepted norm for this type of multi-level marketing business.

The few that remained did well and grossed above average incomes, driving them to greater levels of achievement. Many became regional heads. The company even had norms that allowed successful regional heads grossing certain revenue levels to become individual business owners and have their own individual teams, like a franchisee. As business owners, they were entitled to a permanent commission based on sales achieved by their downstream teams. Owners could move through three levels of directorship based on business acquired. Some directors grossed over half a million USD a year.

In this scenario, a young agent joined the company when he was 22 and grew well. In fact, he was seen as being better than most at the national level. In 20 years, by the time he was 42, he became a director earning over half a million USD a year. He was looked up to by many of his juniors and considered a role model by the company leaders. At this stage, he suddenly found his business slowing down and almost stagnating. He applied all the methods he had learnt and which had proven successful in the past to increase his business, but results were not commensurate with efforts put in.

After a year of limited success, he decided to take a step back and review his journey. He found that he had been highly motivated by his superiors in their group sessions. One of the main motivational drivers being the senior leaders sharing their success stories and inviting others from different groups to share theirs. The message had been a consistent "if we can do it, you can do it", and had always boiled down to "put in more effort, hone your sales skills, keep your eyes on the dollar benefits of achievement, and you'll get there", but there had been no talk on how to build strategies and assess the market or on how to guide one's team towards reaching its full potential. Consequently, as local sales territories got saturated, each team's success waned and their motivational levels dropped.

The star agent realised that merely motivating team players with corporate jargon like "if you want something bad enough, you will find a way to get it", did not achieve the desired results. Basic skills development and motivation are all very good but, in a larger context, a director needs to carve out a marketing strategy for continuous expansion into new territories so his agents' business hit or close rate remained consistently high.

He then began to study the market and interact with directors of other non-competing organisations for ideas on how to identify and develop new markets. He worked on selectively recruiting the right type of agents who specialized and focused on specific product groups. He found that the initial cross selling approach encouraged an unproductive and chaotic free-for-all team environment. This observation motivated him to develop separate strategies for each product stream.

In short, he began to function as the director he had become and not act as the agent he had been trained to be. He moved his business forward slowly but steadily after a two-year dip. He came back with full force as he learnt that corporate managements only train you to a certain level, after which you have to develop yourself. 'Self-development', which is contextual and situational, is the key to success. Today, he is happily on his way to the next level of directorship.

> *Message: Everyone helps you to a point, after which you have to help yourself. It is important to be observant of the world around you in order to continuously learn from others. This way, you get many and different ideas that could help in self upgradation.*

## Case 5: Role success is a context-driven factor

A large multinational consultancy firm, KITI, with revenue over US$ 12 billion, had clients all over the world, with some of the larger clients contributing between US$ 100-600 million each. Overall, a few large clients accounted for 60 per cent of its total business. The consultancy was known for its technical excellence and operational efficiency. Technical capability formed the basis for promoting people to senior positions. Each large client was serviced by an account manager (AM) in charge of the client's business, supported by a relationship manager (RM) who looked after client relations and sales, and a delivery manager (DM) who provided technical services to the client. AMs allotted to smaller clients managed the client business as well as sales, supported only by a DM. Being a technically oriented company, DMs with strong technical backgrounds were promoted as RMs once they received basic training in sales and marketing. Successful RMs were then promoted to AMs. AMs reported to vice presidents who, in turn, reported to the business division head.

Client proposals were usually worked on by a technical team and jointly presented to clients by the RMs and DMs together with technical experts (also called subject matter experts – SME). The AMs and top management would only involve themselves in big deals.

In one particular case, the consultancy firm made an exception when they hired a purely sales-driven local person, James, in Europe as an AM for one of its smaller clients. James had no technical background, but an exceptional track record in winning business deals. Considering the deviation from the standard promotion practice, the business division head took him directly under his wing to ensure he received the support he required from all the departments. James worked hard and grew the business from US$ 5 million to US$ $150 million in 4 years. The KITI management was happy as the results spoke for themselves.

The client who operated in a well-organized and structured manner, was up-to-date with the technology used in their industry and knew what it wanted with specific budgets and clear vendor performance measures laid down. They were also very happy with James because he had an uncanny ability to identify client needs and accordingly align the consultancy's proposals for mutual benefit.

In the fifth year, however, the client's management changed and so did their style of functioning. This led to some minor fissures between James and the client. Though the situation was not so serious, KITIs senior management was able to observe the strain in the relationship. At the same time, James needed to shift to another country in Europe for his son's college education and other personal matters. The KITI management saw this as an opportunity to kill two birds with one stone. They transferred James to the location of his choice and appointed another AM who was a good fit for the client and its current management. However, in this transition James had to accept a client RMs role as this was the only position available at the preferred location. On the other hand, the client had multiple operating bases in different continents and was much larger than the one he serviced earlier. Also, in the new role he reported to the client AM based in India.

Initially, all seemed well but it soon became apparent to the KITI management that its solution had not been the best fit. It was the case of a role change without proper capability and experience alignment. James had become used to independently managing a client and running things his own way. Moreover, he had got used to preferential treatment from in-house departments like administration and human resources as he had reported directly to the divisional head while other AMs had to manage these interfaces on their own. The new role demanded a social and behavioural change which he found most difficult to handle. Earlier 'Subject Matter Experts' reported to him and now they were his peers. James had to upgrade his knowledge and skills to interface better with his peers.

To compound matters further, James found that the new client he had to work with did not operate in a well-organised and structured manner as did his earlier client. There were many instances when the negotiations he held with client leaders were negated by their higher-ups; terms and conditions were often revisited; and budgets committed were revised on a regular basis. The shift from a mature, professional client to an unstructured one demanded a wider range of skills -- from direct selling to strategic planning – some of which he lacked. This impacted his confidence. James found himself in a dilemma as to whether he should ask for another transfer or work on developing himself. The choice became more difficult as he was 50 years old and quite set in his ways. He opted for another transfer.

Having contributed well to the organisation in the past a temporary role was carved out for him. He was asked to provide presales support for major proposals across all product and service streams of the company. He is performing well in this new role.

> *Message: When transitioning 'role-fit' assessment is the key. At senior levels it is important that the stakeholders, the management and the incumbent, should take responsibility to ensure a proper fit. Ignoring this could be detrimental to all concerned.*

## Chapter 2

# Managing Contribution Perceptions

### Introduction

Important stakeholders, power centres and influencers in every dynamic organisation are continuously -- consciously or unconsciously -- observing the contributions of others in the organisation. Their perceptions play an important role when advice is sought; work is allocated; portfolios are restructured; and above all, when promotions and transfers are done. You therefore need to nurture the perceptions others have of you with care, especially those that matter. Contribution perception management is important but usually not paid much attention to by high performers. If incorrect perceptions are formed by key people, not only could your performance suffer, but it could also impact your career path. To illustrate how perception matters, consider this situation. A junior manager makes a suggestion that could solve a problem, but others don't take it seriously as they believe the person may not have the requisite knowledge and experience. However, when a senior manager makes the same suggestion, all accept it. The acceptance is based on perception of the two managers. Another example: When finance managers speak to sales managers about reducing discounts and increasing margins, their suggestions are not accepted because sales managers often believe that finance does not know the nuances of the market. People align themselves, follow and support leaders whom they believe in. This belief is based on their perception. Building the right perception to get others to accept your point of view takes time and effort.

Most successful executives tend to be key contributors in their group. Lower down the ladder, managing contribution perceptions is relatively easy as it is measured on hard facts and evidence on the ground. It follows the old school of thought, which is "keep your nose down, work hard, and you will grow". People always notice one who works hard at lower levels of management but managing contribution perceptions becomes increasingly important to move ahead at senior management levels. This is because the higher you go, you find contribution perceptions are based on subjective parameters to a large extent. At higher levels, decisions are often based on several assumptions made after considering compromises and trade-offs. Examples could range from cost of penetration into new markets, revenue-margin ratios or hiring of a highly competent manager by breaking pay grade norms. Besides this balancing, the different agendas of involved stakeholders whose perception matters, is important.

A key aspect of perception management to keep in mind is that different people assess the same person differently. The board's perception of a CEO will differ from the perception of the CEOs reporting VPs. The powerful stakeholders on the board often form perceptions about a key contributor without personally being in touch with him or her; they rely on the feedback from others. Thus, there are two degrees of separation between the perceivers whose opinion matters and the contributor. Hence creating the right perception in them becomes more difficult. Contributors often have to manage two contextual scenarios to create the desired perception.

This argument can be taken further to cover other scenarios. It is a serious misconception to believe that senior management and owners are the only evaluators of your contribution. Juniors perceive the contribution of their seniors as do VPs of their CEOs. In addition, contribution perception of executives is made by external agency managements. Important external stakeholders whose perceptions matter could be: mission critical monopoly product suppliers, large clients or dealers. Example: Feedback from a large automotive dealer who has the ear of the Chairman could have an impact on the contribution perception of the CEO. While contribution perceptions from external agencies are sometimes taken very seriously it is important to appreciate that they are based on a different set of parameters. These parameters, based on their interface with the organisation, could be related to aspects like delivery, service, fairness and flexibility.

*Summary: Multiple factors are considered while evaluating contribution and the set of factors used by different stakeholders varies according to the perceiver's context. Hence, perception management is complex, important and cannot be left to chance. It often calls for much energy, skill and insight to maintain a delicate balance in managing contribution perceptions made against different contextual backgrounds both within and outside the organisation.*

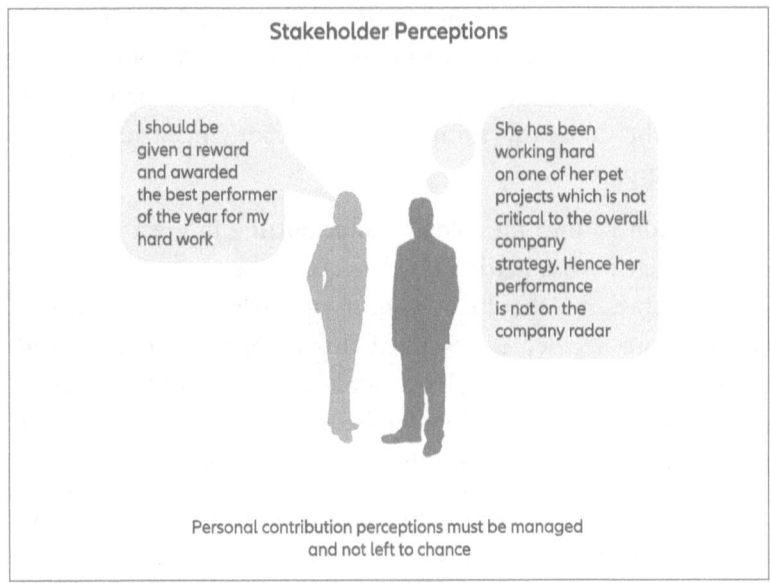

Stakeholder Perceptions

I should be given a reward and awarded the best performer of the year for my hard work

She has been working hard on one of her pet projects which is not critical to the overall company strategy. Hence her performance is not on the company radar

Personal contribution perceptions must be managed and not left to chance

## Managing Contribution Perceptions
## Case Studies

### Case 1: Realign strengths to manage contribution perceptions

A senior manager of a major multinational based in India was posted to the US to take charge as an Account Manager for one of its top 10 clients. The senior manager had put in close to 20 years of service with the company and was well indoctrinated. In his current position he managed the delivery of multiple large projects. He was technically very strong and his interaction with clients was much appreciated as he was able to provide clients with innovative solutions to meet their needs. He was considered a right fit for the role as he was perceived as a solution provider and this would meet the new client's needs.

After a tenure of three years, he was posted back to India as was the company policy. After exploring various roles for this successful manager, the company decided to give him the charge of a new business line which had significant growth potential. The company's senior management, based on several research surveys done by the company think tank, were convinced of the new business opportunity.

Six months into the role and after putting in great effort, the manager felt he was getting nowhere. After several discussions he got the impression that he was not in sync with the management. He therefore decided to leave. At this time, a small competitor (a family owned company) was looking for a CEO who could streamline their organization for better delivery efficiency. They picked up this manager who they thought fit the bill.

In three years, the manager streamlined the delivery operations and improved the talent management. The company grew in leaps and bounds. The client and board were very happy and rewarded the CEO handsomely. However, after that, the Chairman felt that the company growth was slowing down. Every quarter was just showing incremental growth.

After some deliberation with the board, the Chairman spoke to the CEO and asked him to concentrate only on Marketing, Finance, HR and Administration and that they would hire a new senior person to manage the delivery operations. The CEO saw this as a personal growth opportunity so he readily agreed. A new person was hired and a circular was sent to inform all about the change in roles and responsibilities.

In the next 18 months, the business did not grow and some clients were lost. Business relations with the clients deteriorated and new business was brought in at lower margins. This left very little room for error. The operations head began coming under strain as errors, that were earlier covered up, began to get highlighted. This affected the bottom line. On the other hand, the CEO who was very strong technically constantly pointed out the drawbacks in operations management. The operations head also started pointing fingers about the lack of the right skilled people, referencing the CEO's talent management portfolio. The whole situation was very strained and slowly got out of control.

The Chairman and board had several meetings with the CEO and the operations head but were unable to bring about any positive collaboration between the two. They found that managers at the second level on both sides were taking aggressive stands against each other. Finally, the board took a decision to let the CEO go as they felt he was the wrong fit for the current portfolio.

What the CEO did not realize is that in his new role the success parameter was business development. He had taken on the challenge of managing the marketing and business development function, which was not an area of his strength. The board knew that his strengths were in the areas of technology and operations management and that the CEO had used these strengths to bring the company to the current successful state. The CEO's past track record prompted the board to give him a chance to grow into the new role and achieve success over time. From their point of view, it was a reasonable expectation.

The CEO could have focused on projecting his expertise as a 'Solution Provider' to the clients and internally to the sales and marketing team. This would have helped him to bring in more and better-quality business. At the same time, he could also have motivated his sales team by helping in bridging the gap between sales and delivery as both these functions were usually at loggerheads when difficult proposals were to be made. This would have gained him the confidence of both the sales and delivery, which, in turn, would have projected him as the leader that the board was looking for. If he had worked on this change in the perception of his contribution, he would have been in alignment with the board's expectations. Sometimes, it is important to step back and look at the playing field to assess how you are faring and where you stand.

> *Message: In taking on new roles it is important to identify the changed success parameters. This would help to align strengths to manage contribution perception and also deliver to meet expectations.*

## Case 2: Contribution Perceptions – Knowing when to change

A large engineering multinational corporation with a turnover of US$20 billion had several collaborations and joint ventures with reputed international players. They operated through several business streams. As part of a backward integration initiative, they decided to manufacture some base products of which 20% would be for captive use and 80% would be sold in the open market. For the company, this was an aggressive project with a big-ticket budget of over $500 million.

Satisfied with the feasibility report and the broad project plans the board gave its approval to go ahead with the implementation. One of the senior vice presidents (SVP) who had been with the company for over three decades and who had a successful track record of setting-up a number of small plants was selected as the business head for this new subsidiary.

The commissioning took three years and everything moved very well on schedule and according to budget. The board was very happy with the progress. However, no one was keeping an eye on market developments related to regulations on import and export as well as new innovations taking place. After this initiative was approved, all eyes were focused on getting the project to go live.

Suddenly, as the project was about to go live, the market took a turn and the market value of the signature product crashed by

60%. This was due to material price changes based on global inter-government agreements and also because of some disruptive innovations by competitors. The project became unviable.

The company went into damage control mode. However, even after 18 months, there was no sign of getting the project to become viable but the board insisted on hanging on to the initiative as losses were being covered by other major business streams. They felt that the situation would ease in time.

At this stage, the project was four and a half years old and the selected SVP who was a top performer in his previous roles began to get nervous. He had a contract with the company to retain 100% bonus for the first three years during commissioning and, following that, the bonus was to be decided based on an agreed business performance.

When the market changed, the board and the MD negotiated a 75% bonus for the next two years with the SVP. The SVP then started losing confidence in the revival of the project. He realized that the management was hanging on to the initiative to manage the shareholders' expectations and were waiting for an appropriate time to announce the closure of the project. To the SVP, this would take another year.

He then decided to approach the management with a proposal for another role so his contribution could be among the top performers as before. However, there was no role at the same level available in the company and they said he would have to settle for another position that would not have been in his core strength area.

The SVP then decided to leave, as the current project would have affected his track record. Further, salvaging the current project would not have been appreciated by his current or future employers. He left the company with good feelings and moved on to another challenging role where his contribution would be recognized for the positive results he brought to the new company. All entities involved appreciated the separation and wished the SVP well in his future career endeavors.

Overall, the SVP retained his contribution perception in the company and market. At the same time, he gained the goodwill of all concerned.

> *Message: It is important to know when to cut your losses in a timely manner, especially when you are a victim of circumstances. Keeping abreast with other stakeholder motives is a must in general. However, for critical situations such as this a higher degree of alertness helps.*

## Case 3: Seizing opportunities - Changing perceptions

In one of the medium sized armies (about 70,000 troops) in the world, a brilliant young infantry officer rose rapidly through the ranks and became a Formation Commander ahead of his batch mates. He was an outstanding leader and motivated the troops under his command to achieve tasks beyond their normal capacity. He, however, had a bias towards the combat arms. He also felt that the technical and service branches of the armed forces were not working optimally and could deliver much more than they were doing at present.

Under his command, he had a technical branch head who worked well but did not go out of his way to improve the status quo. The Formation Commander often felt that the combat forces would be compromised if the technical support did not get upgraded. When questioned, the branch head gave several excuses which included, budgets, red tape, lack of training and manpower besides others. Though this frustrated the Formation Commander he continued to search for a way to improve the situation.

At this time, the transfer orders of the technical head were received. The Formation Commander decided to take up a different approach with the new technical head. Being a true leader, he called in the new head for a discussion. The main focus was to impress upon the new head that a marked improvement was needed to strengthen the technical support to the combat forces. The new head, a highly motivated officer was keen on making a difference. After the discussion, he studied the state of affairs in the technical branches under his responsibility for a week and went back to the Formation Commander with a plan to do an audit of all technical equipment and installations at the 30 odd different locations under his supervision. The Formation Commander because of his past dealings with the previous technical head, was not happy with the proposal and didn't expect much from the audit. As he had low expectations and there was not much to lose, he reluctantly gave the officer permission to go ahead with his audit and get back to him with a time-bound plan within two months.

The officer set out and visited installation by installation, met the technicians, reviewed their living conditions, inspected the equipment and most of all collected the technical and personal concerns of the people on the ground. This was a difficult task as the installations were situated along 200 miles of the border area, in high altitude mountainous terrain where the weather conditions were severe. When he came back with a detailed report of the 'As-Is' situation and his proposed 'To-be' plan, the Formation Commander was impressed. This was the first step in breaking the ice between the two. It brought about a change in the perception of the technical head's contributions.

The Formation Commander and the technical head then started working together to mitigate the constraints of red tape, budgets and to an extent, the politics involved in getting things done. Initially, things moved slowly, but after some time, momentum picked up and people began to believe that things could change. The technical head worked very hard, often deviated from laid-down processes and even broke chain of command to get the new equipment released. He then ensured its transportation and installation besides arranging for the training of his men. Seeing this, many began to pitch in to support the technical improvement drive. The men on the ground too got motivated to stretch themselves in order to make things happen ahead of time. Soon the perception of the technical branches changed in the eyes of the combat forces and their contribution was recognized and appreciated by all. The Formation Commander commended the technical head for his contribution and recommended him for a promotion.

In this case, the new technical head not only enhanced his contribution to the command but also changed the perception that the combat troops had of the technical branches. The seniors in the technical branches also recognized and appreciated this. When the proposal for his next promotion came up, he got the support of all. Personal attitude is also a major factor in managing perception.

---

*Message: Contribution perceptions can be managed by being alert and seizing opportunities. Justifying status quo does not help when management is looking for improvement. In addition, we see that in this case, when a leader stretches not only does his team extend themselves but others from outside get motivated to pitch in.*

---

## Case 4: Managing expected contribution perceptions

About twenty years ago, a large multinational corporation headquartered in Europe decided to expand in India. The corporation was world renowned and a leader in the range of products they produced. When the company set up shop in India they sent an operations specialist as the first managing director (MD-1). His mandate was to set-up and run the plant to set targeted outputs.

When MD-1 came to India, he focused on commissioning the machines and setting up production layouts. He worked hard and made the managers and workers work long hours. He was a good leader and motivated his people well with incentives, bonuses and overtime compensation. The people were happy and all targets and plans went on schedule. However, the cost of production was 7% above normal which did not alarm the headquarters due to the low cost of production in India. However, the quality was acceptable by Indian standards but below the European quality standards. Hence, products could not be exported. MD-1's belief was that conformance to performance was more important than conformance to design. So, if quality met local user standards it was OK. This too did not raise a red flag at the head office.

Based on the agreed tenure plan, MD-1 was transferred in three years. He was handsomely rewarded and given a choice posting. He had met the contribution perception of the management.

At this stage, the European corporation sent a Quality specialist as MD-2. His main contribution was to ensure that the quality of output met global standards for export and that the quality produced for the Indian market was above the local standards. MD-2 was very firm and did not allow products with deviation. He often did this at the cost of delayed deliveries. He believed that conformance to design was as important as conformance to performance. His theory was that the design covered a wider scope of product usage and hence the return of defective products from the field would be considerably less. This had been scientifically proved by company researchers. To change the quality culture in the Indian subsidiary was a difficult task. With the introduction of several training programs and incentive schemes MD-2 managed to deliver quality products as per the plan. In fact, he was able to get the parent company to transfer a few product lines to India where global requirements were too small to be economically manufactured in Europe. MD-2 met the contribution perception expectations of the head office and was rewarded handsomely. He however was unable to manage the production costs that rose from an overrun of 7% to 10%. MD-2 was transferred after his three-year tenure.

MD-3 who replaced MD-2 had a finance background. His role was to contain costs and make the operations more profitable. He audited the operations and started many waste reduction campaigns, held people responsible for tool usage, consumable consumption and worked on reduction in other high cost areas. Initially, there was a fear in the local company that he would cut wages and reduce bonuses, however after he gave the employees an assurance that their income would not be affected he got the full cooperation of all and was able to almost achieve his target. The cost overrun dropped from 10% to 3%. MD-3 convinced the management that this achievement was significant considering the difficult situation and change in the material procurement costs. The management recognized his contribution and also rewarded him appropriately.

MD-3 left India after his tenure of three years and the next MD, an Indian, who had considerable experience of working in a European MNC in India, replaced him.

The main learning here is that all MDs had some deviation from the overall company norms such as; quality, delivery and costs. However, the parent company management appreciated their contribution as they met the expectations for which they were selected. Even if an MD improved on any other parameter but did not achieve their expected contribution they would not have been commended as much by their management. Managing expected contribution perceptions is important as it also gives the people that selected the MDs the satisfaction of making good decisions with the right judgement.

*Message: Managing Contribution perceptions requires focused dedication to the main goal. Getting distracted when other parameters are slightly compromised does not help. In addition, it is important to remember that focusing on parameters that are not on the expectation scanner does not give you brownie points when performance is below par.*

## Case 5: Mismatch of contribution perceptions can backfire

A large multinational IT corporation headquartered in India had sent one of its senior managers to take charge of a major US client. The business with this client was substantial and was one of the MNCs top 10 accounts. The account was having some delivery problems and a senior manager (SM) with a track record of resolving such problems was put in charge.

The SM did well and, within one year, he set things right and started working on building relationships and growing the business. In three years, when it was time for the SM to return to India, the client insisted that the SM be kept on for another year. This suited the MNC as the client budget for IT in the next year was significant. All went well and the SM brought the MNC considerable business. The SM's contribution to the company and client was well appreciated as it matched their perceptions.

On his return to India, the MNC was searching for a position for the SM, who had now been made a VP. Before he left India, he was working in Mumbai and was familiar with the region. However, there was no vacancy in western India so he was put into a position as the Vice Regional Head in south India. This position was unattractive to him because of its administrative component but the delivery responsibility that was attached made the job acceptable.

Soon, the newly promoted VP found that the Head of the southern region had a different way of functioning and began to sideline him for many important decisions. The top management knew the value of the VP and tried to give him some initiatives where he would directly report to the MD. This worked for some time, but the strain of dual reporting along with confusing and make-shift goals had taken its toll on the VP. At this time, the head of the Eastern region retired. The MD decided to give the post to the VP. This would help to fill the vacancy with a good person and at the same time reduce the frustrations of a valuable asset.

The VP took up the position in Kolkata, a place where he had never worked before. The position was more administrative with very little direct exposure to projects. He worked hard for six months but was not getting anywhere. The culture was different and most of the work progressed slowly. He often spent long hours in the office but could get very few others to work with him. Also, most work was uninteresting to him. He mentioned this to the MD who thought it was a teething problem and the VP would get over it in time.

After nine months, the VP suddenly resigned and took over as CEO of an Indian start up subsidiary of a European IT MNC. This subsidiary was being set up in south India. Being very familiar with the local work culture and the local talent available he did very well and soon began to take on higher global roles. His contribution exceeded the expectations of the top management and he was well rewarded.

The Indian MNC was unable to truly understand the reason for the sudden departure. After other experiences over a few years, they came to realize that the mismatch of experience and capabilities linked to positions cannot be treated lightly. Putting a person in a senior position does not curtail the frustration of low contribution because of environmental and other parameters. High performers are constantly concerned about their contribution to the company. When the 'position-capability' mismatch prevents them from performing at the high levels they are accustomed to, they often opt out. It has been observed that high performers who are in market demand often leave to retain their edge when their current organization role does not allow them higher achievement opportunities.

> *Message: Managing contribution perceptions is a two-way process. Both management and managers need to understand the seriousness of this and be alert enough to take timely action. Capability and cultural fit are also an important consideration for transitioning. This is besides the ability to manage the organizational dynamics in the new role.*

## Chapter 3

# Managing the Ecosystem

### Introduction

Entrepreneurs, CEOs and senior managers who wish to succeed, must cooperate and collaborate with one another and other external bodies to meet their organisational goals. This seems very simple in theory but it is complex and difficult to manage when put into actual practice. An ecosystem may be described as a galaxy of stakeholders that influence desired outcomes that the CEO or senior manager is trying to achieve.

To facilitate the smooth functioning of an organisation, management circulates policies and processes as guidelines for day-to-day decisions. By definition, "a policy is a single decision for a frequently occurring issue or problem". However, life is not all that simple; else, organisations would run on policies alone. Organisational policies and processes can never be followed in totality – As the saying goes "work to rule is a strike". This means that if one follows the book of rules in totality nothing will work. This is because it is very difficult to cover all situations through policies. Policies evolve over a period of time as situations are experienced. Some policies are added and others are dropped based on the changing times. Senior managers have to continuously use their discretionary power to take decisions in areas calling for deviation from policy. This may often have ramifications on other stakeholders.

In actual practice, we find each department has its own agenda (strategies and performance matrices) and goals which often work against each other. This is seen in the contradictory matrices between purchase, finance, sales and warehousing. Example: Purchase might want to order bulk quantities for better rates while finance is reluctant to release funds to manage cash flow effectively and warehousing would be aiming for more turns in inventory.

Many misalignments exist due to the differing agendas of the stakeholders; some are caused by the structure and systems of the organisation itself. This is seen where systems are designed to facilitate greater operational control or efficiency but simultaneously cramp the freedom of others. This is particularly true for those in business acquisition who need to constantly adapt to meet market demand and dynamics. Some of these are sales discounts which are based on the competition pricing strategies. Others could be rerouting distribution based on the supply and demand situation. Hence managing the ecosystem across departments calls for relationship management that would help to work out mutually acceptable compromises and trade-offs.

Besides agenda misalignments, another aspect to be considered in managing the ecosystem is a power centre shift in an organisation. This can be due to market dynamics or management strategy changes. In some cases, we see functions such as finance, R&D, industrial engineering and marketing would need to change their ecosystem management strategies to align with the new internal situations. An example would be when a company's monopoly status changes due the entry of a competitor. As a monopoly the power centre would generally be the manufacturing function (the more you produce the more you sell). When a competitor enters the market the sales becomes the power center as getting products off the shelves becomes more important than production. Organizational changes also take place due to mergers and acquisitions, government regulatory policy changes, disruptive innovations and other factors as these change the dynamics of business. It is, therefore, essential that senior leaders are continuously tuned into ecosystem dynamics and take timely steps to effectively manage their own ecosystems to adapt to change and navigate through conflicting agendas.

*Summary: Managing ecosystems is an important personal attribute for success in senior management positions. Building trust and working out agenda compromises and trade-offs is the key to ensure that all stakeholders are on board when navigating to achieve personal and organisational goals.*

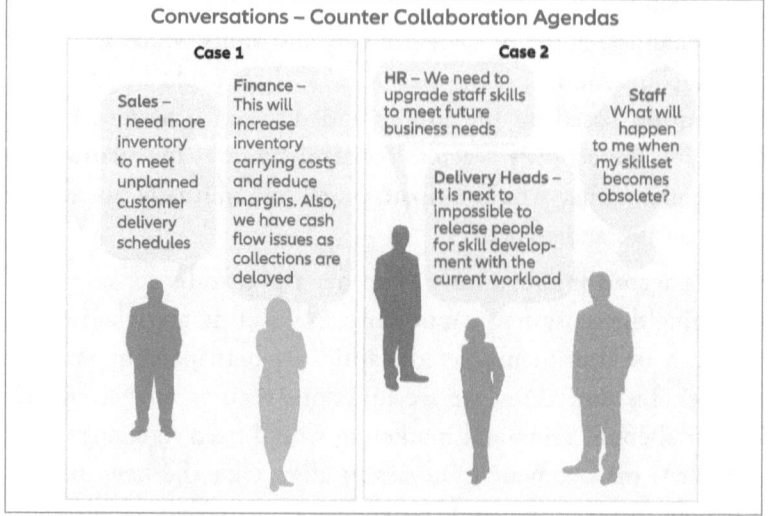

Conversations – Counter Collaboration Agendas

**Case 1**

Sales – I need more inventory to meet unplanned customer delivery schedules

Finance – This will increase inventory carrying costs and reduce margins. Also, we have cash flow issues as collections are delayed

**Case 2**

HR – We need to upgrade staff skills to meet future business needs

Delivery Heads – It is next to impossible to release people for skill development with the current workload

Staff What will happen to me when my skillset becomes obsolete?

## Managing the Ecosystem

## Case Studies

### Case 1: Importance of board comfort in MD selection

A large engineering company, one of the top 50 Fortune 500 companies, had a subsidiary in India. The local company had four streams of business and the normal support functions such as finance, HR and administration.

Four vice presidents headed the four streams and they reported to the managing director who, in turn, was responsible to the board of directors. The board consisted of the Chairman with three executive directors, two independent directors and a non-executive director. The managing director was also on the board.

While the company was doing well and business growth was ahead of targets the four vice presidents' business contribution in profit and revenue to the company was as follows:

| Distribution | VP 1 | VP 2 | VP 3 | VP 4 | Total |
|---|---|---|---|---|---|
| Revenue | 20% | 15% | 40% | 25% | 100% |
| Profit Volume | 18% | 12% | 20% | 50% | 100% |

All other parameters considered more or less equal, it was assumed by most of the senior managers, large suppliers and customers that VP 4 would be the successor to the current MD.

In a couple of years, the MD retired and when the new MD was announced it was VP 3 and not VP 4. This was very surprising to all because VP 4 was responsible for bringing in the highest profit volume. He was also people oriented, business savvy and had a good equation with suppliers and customers besides being well respected by the parent company.

VP 4 was quite upset at first but then settled down and decided to find out as to what went wrong. He got himself a mentor to analyse the situation and identify the reason as to why he was not given the MDs position. After several interactions with VP 4 and others over a few months the mentor was able to find out the reasons as to why VP 4 was not considered for the MDs position.

What came to light was that VP 4 had not built a rapport with the board members or maintained contact with them on a continuous basis. They knew VP 4 based on the figures in the books, the profile that the company provided and a few interactions they had with the VPs over the years.

This was not so for VP 3 who had built a rapport with most of the directors by sharing information, seeking advice and meeting them at various functions outside the company. VP 3 made it a point to understand the interests of each director and their specialization and used all opportunities to share information on areas of interest and seek guidance in their area of specialization. Over time, VP 3 built a relationship with the directors where they felt comfortable dealing with him.

When the time came to select the next MD, the obvious choice was VP 3. People like to deal with those they know and are comfortable with and would be willing to compromise on a few points of merit in other areas provided all factors were more or less equal.

This revelation to VP 4 was an eye opener because it dawned on him that merit points in performance are not the only factor at higher levels. Relationships as well as building a comfort zone within the ecosystem are important.

The mentor helped VP 4 to develop a plan in order to build relationships with the directors while maintaining his performance.

VP 4 diligently followed the plan for a few years. When the current MD left for greener pastures after three years, VP 4 became the automatic choice. Today, after five years in the MD position, VP 4 has been promoted to head one of the major regions of the world for the parent company.

> *Message: Managing ecosystems is based on building relationships. This helps build comfort zones that facilitate working relationships. The ecosystem management process also helps to build a sense of inclusiveness towards achieving overall goals.*

## Case 2: Performance and people management are inclusive

A large non-profit organization that has close to a 100,000 employees working in different divisions across the world successfully implements programs in a number of countries.

One of its several divisions had major operations in four countries, each headed by a vice president (VP). The setup had all the general departments of which one was the program management office (PMO) that was also managed by a VP. The PMO monitored the programs in different countries and provided support and guidance where required.

During the course of regular operations, the directors found that VP, Ramis, handling the PMO function was very effective. He always asked the right questions, put programs back on track and seemed to have an acumen for detecting early warning signals of programs that were inclined towards failure.

One of the programs (PM-X1) was not doing too well and in spite of repeated interventions from the head office, things could not be set right. After watching the situation for over nine months the directors at the head office decided to send Ramis who was heading the PMO function to take over the operations in that country. This took place in the 4th Quarter of 2011.

Ramis handled the new position very well. He systematically broke down the power centers that were disrupting the program, established systems to monitor progress and efficiency and developed methods to incentivize work at the execution level. Things fell into place and the performance of the PM-X1 program grew dramatically. However, one thing that the VP did not take into consideration was the human element vis-à-vis acceptance of the pace of change and the emotional stress caused by the changed power systems. This left many people unhappy. Most issues for him were resolved objectively and rationally. This way he steamrolled the opposition.

The directors were very happy with his performance over 15 months and decided to transfer him to another region to shape up another program (PM-X2) that was flagging. This was in January 2013.

Ramis, took over the operations of (PM-X2) and went about it in the same way as (PM-X1) and by the first quarter of 2014 everything was going well for this program too.

It was time for Ramis to be transferred again and all thought that he would be in great demand because of his successes. However, to their surprise there were no takers. Even at the corporate office the individual directors were not too happy to have him on their team.

It finally became apparent that the directors had used Ramis as a 'fix-it' resource who did the work well but left a trail of ill feelings. Most people were not too keen to work with him as he did not have the requisite emotional sensitivity for the position he held. In other words, he was unable to manage the ecosystem.

Ramis was finally called back to headquarters and given a staff function that was advisory in nature and had very little interface with executors.

Initially Ramis was most upset and felt he had been used. However, it took time for him to realize that performance must be coupled with ecosystem management. He is now trying to rectify his approach towards problem resolution. Though it will take time to change perceptions, many feel he will get there as his intentions were always good. He however, will have to learn that when people get hurt, they are extra cautious with the person in their future dealings. Building goodwill is more difficult and time consuming when your track record speaks otherwise.

> *Message: At higher levels end result performance factors are important. However if considered in isolation it has been found that these wins are short term and not sustainable. An unhappy team with good results does not last long. Hence, balancing performance with sensitivity to ecosystem management is important for sustainable success.*

## Case 3: Managing mission critical contributors

A new CEO was appointed in a large engineering services company. She had excellent technical and delivery skills besides being fairly competent in other general areas. She was an internal candidate and an obvious choice.

When she took up the position, business went on as usual and she felt she had a grip on the situation and that the company was poised for growth. There were one or two resignations of senior subject matter specialists but nothing to lose sleep over as the level below was good and had been groomed well to take charge.

The organizational structure was such that about 20 managers officially reported to the CEO. The organization had 250,000 employees and operated in 30 countries. The company had 10 different business streams that had separate responsibilities, five regional business and marketing heads and about eight support functions such as finance, administration, human resources, R&D

and so on. This was on paper. However, in actual practice, over 50 senior executives regularly interacted with the CEO and claimed that they were reporting to her. These were highly talented managers who were in demand in the market. The former CEO had the charisma to manage these people in such a way that they gave their best and remained with the company. The new CEO soon found that the actual functioning of the company was different from what was laid down in the official structure.

Most people outside the organization chart that said they reported to the CEO were the heads of different 'Centres of Excellence' (COE). COEs were small R&D centres that specialized in a domain, technology or product. They researched and provided solutions to specific customer-reported problems or where projects under the delivery function needed support in resolving technical problems. The COEs were part of a differential and cutting-edge service that the company provided to customers. The heads were high performing contributors with a low profile in the media but well known to the competition. All competitors were constantly trying to poach these COE heads. This made it very important for the company to retain them and keep them happy.

The new CEO soon realized that her role included managing these COE heads who were an integral part of the ecosystem and who also played an important role for organisational success. She studied them individually and found a common thread running through all apart from a few variants.

They all had big egos, were vying for leadership in their community of specialists and wanted an audience for exposure. Besides this, they wanted support to file for patents as well as publish and present white papers at reputable platforms.

The new CEO, after studying the situation, provided the specialists with the support and resources that they needed. She also provided them leads for appropriate exposure and at the same time used them to promote the image of the company. In this way, she kept good people with the company and also used them to grow the business.

The new CEO was well respected as she adapted to the formal and informal organizational needs of the organisation. Managing the ecosystem took much of her time and energy but the results were more than encouraging. Eventually she turned out to be a very successful CEO and a model to many.

---

*Message: Ecosystems need to be managed across structures and boundaries. Sensitivity to the human element in business operations often becomes the key to success. While ecosystem management is important at all levels the impact of mismanagement is greater at higher levels. This makes it one of the most important skill requirements for persons in top positions.*

---

## Case 4: Managing incompetent senior executives

A large multinational conglomerate based in India, had many subsidiaries and joint-venture (JV) companies. These businesses covered several sectors like manufacturing, power, IT, engineering services, aviation and others. Some of the subsidiaries and JVs had overlapping businesses and customers. This led to minor issues which had to be sorted out at the corporate level. A few of the companies came under the engineering services sector. In this sector, the MD was due to retire in one of the larger companies.

The company had two VPs, Ron and Joe, that were vying for the position. Both were competent in their respective streams. Ron was technical and delivery focused and Joe was business and people oriented. The board had to choose one or the other but found that they were reluctant to report to each other. If one was selected the other would leave. After wrestling with the problem for some time, the board decided to make Joe the MD and transfer Ron as an MD to another subsidiary in a similar line of business. Though the subsidiary would be smaller in size, it had the flavour of a multinational JV. This was because the subsidiary started as a JV partnership between a US company and its Indian counterpart. The US partner had been bought out by the Indian group some years ago.

Both Ron and Joe were satisfied with the board's decision. The board members were very pleased with themselves because they felt that they killed two birds with one stone besides this, the subsidiary was not doing so well and often had issues with the larger company over client interference. Now that both the MDs had worked together for many years it was expected that the issues would reduce between the companies and the larger company could pass on some business to the subsidiary to help boost its performance. All round the situation looked good.

Ron who took over as MD of the smaller subsidiary had a strong delivery and quality orientation. He went into depth and started sorting out problems related to operational efficiencies and quality. While doing this, he realized that there were quite a few senior executives who had been promoted to levels beyond their competency. After investigation, he found that in the initial stages of the joint venture, its overseas partner deputed executives from their foreign companies as MDs in India. These MDs from USA had only one objective and that was to get the business running and show short-term results. They came on assignments for about 2 to 3 years and then left. The MDs sent from overseas were from the JV partner's middle management cadre. They were also selected for their specialization in a particular function. For example, the first MD sent after the JV was signed, was a technical specialist. After 3 years when he was posted out, a systems specialist was sent to improve operational efficiency, and after him a marketing-oriented person was sent and so on.

Each of these MDs looked at the organization and promoted people based on current performance and without looking too much into the 'personal growth potential' factor. This was something like promoting a brilliant engineer with low potential to become a manager. Ron learnt that he had quite a few senior executives who were passengers but wielded a lot of influence in the organization. These executives had reached their level of incompetence years ago and were now playing a political game to cover their insecurity.

While Ron was able to sort out quite a few problems, the company performance remained dismal. Besides this, complaints to the board increased and the informal rumblings from dissatisfied senior executives (passengers) became louder.

Ron was called several times by the board and was told to bring the situation under control. Each time, he made a case to prove that the incompetent senior executives and their negative influence on the teams, was one of the major factors impacting performance. While the case was very rational, the suggested solutions to remove these people were not accepted. The board felt that sacking senior people would cause a major disruption in the subsidiary apart from being bad for the morale of the executives and also the company's image. They wanted Ron to find a way to work with the old timers. However, the MD was not a people's person and found it difficult to make compromises on the work front.

Finally, after about 18 months Ron was asked to resign. When questioned, the response given by the board was "Unable to manage the passengers". Every company has its own share of passengers and it is part of the MD's job to manage them.

> *Message: Ecosystem management includes management of passengers. These people are often influential communication brokers and can get things done. By building relationships and dispelling their insecurity through trust, passengers can be motivated to use their influencing skills to enhance performance. This would lead to a win-win situation for all.*

## Case 5: Single Client - Multiple stakeholder management

A large utility company in Europe, ASTAR, engaged the services of a multinational engineering services company, ISEI, headquartered in India. The overall expenditure on outsourced engineering services by ASTAR was about a billion euros.

ASTAR initially engaged five engineering services companies from different parts of the world and distributed the work fairly evenly. Over time, they dropped one company and distributed the work such that ISEI had 50% wallet share and the balance was divided among the other three.

ISEI was very good at what they did and, in addition, had a good research wing that came up with a variety of transformational ideas for cost savings. This pleased the President of the utility firm. Though he had a technical bent of mind and could appreciate the innovations that brought in cost reductions and increased efficiency, the most important success factor for him was the financial gains seen in the improved bottom-line. The company rating by the big three credit rating agencies, Moody›s Investors Service, Standard & Poor's (S&P) and Fitch got upgraded. The president also got close to the Indian company because they incubated many of his pet ideas in their R&D labs, some of which turned out to be winners.

While all was going well, ISEI executives were getting closer to the president but did not notice the growing animosity among

ASTARs vice presidents. This was mainly because of the difficulties and tensions they had to go through to implement the changes based on ISEIs suggested innovations. Processes had to be modified, people had to be re-trained, reporting systems needed to be restructured and all this at a pace that the lower level executers found difficult to manage. Hence, the implementation programs had many glitches and the line functions had many sleepless nights. This was besides the mounting tension in the lower level execution teams.

At different points of time, these constraints were brought to the President's notice but they were not taken seriously. He often pushed them aside saying that it was part of growth and change. 'No pain no gain' was his motto.

This scenario continued for about seven years until it was time for the ASTAR President to retire. By this time ASTAR became one of the top five customers of ISEI. The business to ISEI from ASTAR was slightly more than 700 million euros.

Soon after the ASTAR President retired and one of the VPs replaced him, things started changing for ISEI. Regular reviews and audits were set up for all vendors. ISEI was not given any special treatment and was often audited on price and performance parameters more stringently than others. The new president took pleasure in playing hard-ball with ISEI because of the past hardships he had faced. Within three years, ISEI business came down from 700 to 100 million euros

The CEO of ISEI soon realized that there was a relationship deficit between the two companies. ISEI in its enthusiasm to work closely with the past president had ignored the other vice presidents with whom they just maintained a cursory relationship. These vice presidents jointly with the new President systematically cut the business of ISEI to less than 10% of the wallet share.

The lesson learnt in client engagement was taken seriously by ISEI. They set up a team to find out why the business and relationship had deteriorated. In a short while, the team found that the marketing and client engagement executives of the company did not spend time and effort to build rapport with senior members and other power centres of the client. In their enthusiasm to grow the business, they turned a blind eye to the client ecosystem and were unaware of the increasing dissent among the vice presidents. Eventually, ISEI lost the business.

*Message: Managing ecosystems is not only for internal performance achievement. Awareness of ecosystems prevalent in external engagements is equally important for success. In this case it is important to remember that managing the ecosystem through multi-level relationship building engagements with clients, at all times, is important to maintain and sustain business growth.*

## Chapter 4

# Managing Partnership Priorities

### Introduction

Partnerships, in the context of an organization, refer to the collaboration between one or more stakeholders (from within or outside) to achieve common goals.

Many senior executives are practicing partnership prioritization without being aware of it. Those that do it better than others are often not able to reach their full potential because they are unaware of the skills they possess. This lack of awareness prevents them from honing their skills further.

When working on important and mission critical goals, people develop close relationships over time. There is a certain amount of emotional bonding and trust that is built up. This is due to the frequent interactions, shared stresses and strains, common wins and losses, among other things. While these partnerships facilitate higher performance, they however, last only until the goals are achieved. If a new or existing goal brings professionals together, the partnerships continue to grow and strengthen.

In dynamic business situations, change is the constant. Markets change, new strategies are adopted, organization structures change, technologies change, disruptive innovations bring in new products besides other realignments in business partnerships and government regulations. All these lead to changes in professional partnerships. This is other than personal decisions to change one's own path.

Situational changes can lead to a change in goals or the means to a goal. This leads to new stakeholder groups being formed, or even a stakeholder's importance in the same group, may change. This causes people to reprioritize their partnerships. In other words, people need to disengage from existing partners, forge new partnerships or even re-engage with old partners based on the relevance to current situations. The level and depth of engagement may vary based on the situation and the goal.

A partnership bond is developed or nurtured for mutual gains in goal achievement. There is a certain amount of bonding based on mutual trust and understanding of interdependencies. The partnership development process is a focused activity and has three stages – engagement, maintenance and disengagement. All stages take a considerable amount of effort, both mental and physical, besides an investment in time. It is, therefore, not very practical to maintain a large number of partnerships at any point of time. Hence, partnership reprioritization becomes important to maintain effective and mutually beneficial relationships.

A simple example of the need for partnership reprioritization would be when an organization shifts from being market centric to delivery or production centric. Or when an organization shifts from brick and mortar systems to online systems. On the face of it, this may look like an opportunistic approach to partnership building but in actual practice it becomes a necessity. In the case of change from a market centric to a delivery centric organisation, the importance of sales and marketing stakeholders will decrease and that at the production function stakeholders will increase. Hence, management spends more time and energy on the new stakeholders, in this case production heads, on whom the company performance now becomes more dependent. Hence, new bonds are developed and old bonds weaken or fade away as the organisation evolves.

While there is a very rational explanation for engagement and disengagement of partners, in this context termed as 'partnership reprioritization', the emotional factor constrains people from taking the appropriate reprioritization decisions. This often dilutes the effectiveness of a senior executive in the long run. Even partnership disengagements are to be delicately managed to ensure that no negative vibes are created in the process.

A common phenomenon seen in old organizations with a history of changes in stakeholder importance, is that a number of passengers are retained or carried along because of past partnership relations. In fact, many such people can be replaced at half the cost and for double the efficiency, but this is not done and senior management tries to fit them in. This is a good thing to boost the morale of people but when measured in terms of cost balance, the cut-off becomes a difficult decision because of emotional considerations.

*Summary: Managing partnership prioritization is an important consideration for senior managers not only in terms of business goals but also personal effectiveness. The partnership prioritization process is also an area that needs to be developed.*

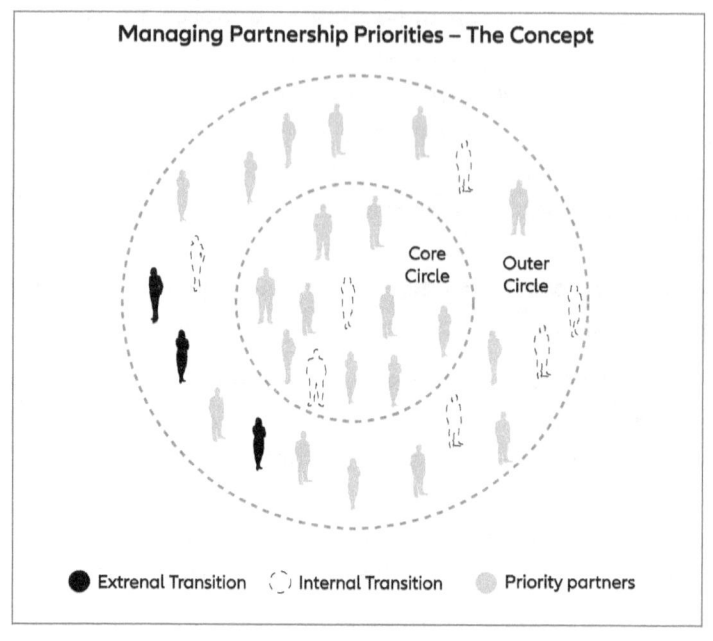

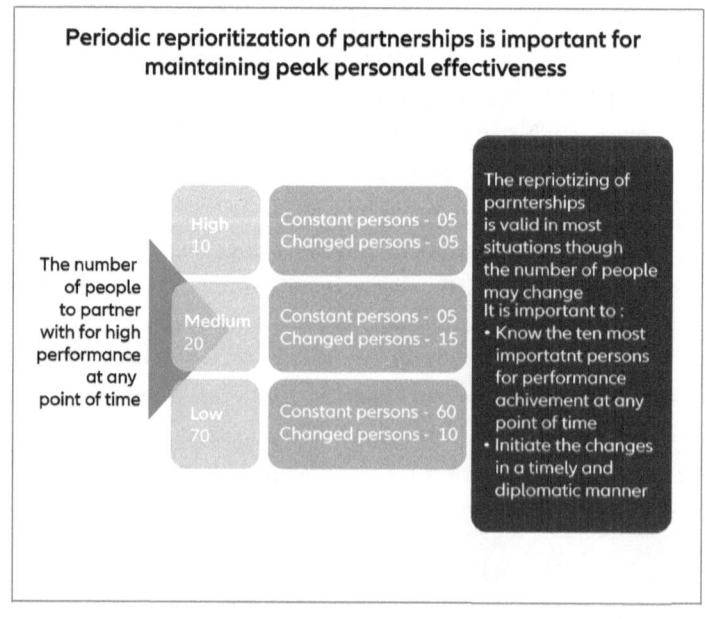

## Managing Partnership Priorities
## Case Studies

### Case 1: MD Partnering with Business Line EVPs

Ram, the MD of a large $15 billion engineering corporation was managing eight major and three small business lines. The business covered a diverse spectrum of industry sectors like power transmission, infrastructure, defense equipment (DE), information technology (IT), heavy engineering, marine engineering, transportation engineering (TE) and aerospace products.

The business divisions were headed by executive vice presidents (EVP) who were known for their competence in specific industry sectors. Ram maintained a good rapport with the EVPs as most of them had been with the company for over 15-20 years.

Over 50% of the business came from the government sector and this was dependent on the programs rolled out by different central and state agencies. Hence, there were peak and slack business periods.

Ram managed his partnership relations with the EVPs based on the intensity and size of the business. He worked closely with the business lines that were in a peak period, had several meetings with the EVPs and their teams and met their customers to promote further business. He would ride the wave and make the most of peak periods.

At these times, he did not ignore the divisions that were in a slack period. He would call for conferences, involve them in new market exploration and R&D projects besides setting some guidelines to prepare for future trends. He spent less than 20% of his time on this and it worked well with some EVPs. However, some EVPs who were accustomed to a close association with the MD and the time he spent with their divisions, were unhappy.

One of the EVPs, Anil, was from the DE business line. He expected Ram to get more involved with defense projects and product trends. He was also instrumental in organizing meetings between Ram and high-level government officials to build relations and explore future business possibilities. Initially Ram obliged but it became a drag on his time. Ram then slowly pulled away and spent time sparingly with the DE group. This had a negative impact on Anil as well as his next level subordinates. Motivation levels dropped as Anil was unable to hold his team together without Ram's motivational presence. Ram noticed this and tried to compensate but it became difficult to manage. He managed to hold the group for 2-3 slack business swings but later he found that Anil had fallen into what is called a 'high maintenance' category. Anil got disheartened and eventually left the company. A new EVP from outside was hired to take over.

Most of the other EVPs were comfortable with Ram's style of functioning and managed their groups well. The infrastructure business EVP, Sunil, was particularly good as he managed the business independently and both he and Ram got on very well. Eventually Sunil became the next MD.

Sunil as MD was keen on developing the IT business division for export, in order to increase foreign exchange earnings. The EVP heading the IT business line could not align with Sunil's growth strategies left the organization. Sunil then recruited an EVP from outside to run the IT business line. The EVP selected was aligned to the MDs business growth strategy. He was an outstanding technocrat with a strong marketing background. He was good at 'wowing' customers and striking large deals. He was an NRI and therefore had the advantage of foreign customer connects and also a good understanding of their needs. However, overall business management was not the EVP's forte. Hence, though business acquisition was good, the execution and business management were below the company's operating norms. Sunil had to spend much time to nurture the newly recruited EVP and other IT business group team members to formulate a viable business model. Though the IT business line was not making a loss, it did not grow as expected and the margins were below the industry norms.

Sunil inducted his best people, those who had a proven track record across business lines in the parent company, to support the new EVP, but to no avail. Both sides were unable to arrive at workable win-win partnership because of the different backgrounds they came from and also their resistance to change. Rigid stances on both sides led to unviable working relationships. Over a period of eight years, Sunil changed four IT division EVPs as he could not build the required partnership with any of them or between the EVPs and their teams. He also found it difficult to get the new EVPs aligned to the parent company business model. Sunil eventually had to sell off the IT business under pressure from the board.

---

*Message: Partnering prioritization management is not always successful and does not work in all situations. Cultural and experiential backgrounds besides the degree of resistance to change impact partnering. Also, it is important to appreciate that business models that are successful in one industry may not be viable in another. Forcing an engineering business model on to IT may not have been the right approach.*

---

## Case 2: Keeping links open when priorities change

A medium sized family-owned construction company, AP & Sons, (APS) was doing well according to industry standards. Their quality was among the top five in the industry and their delivery was mostly on schedule. They were able to manage their customers' expectations by providing services that delighted them at marginal additional costs.

APS had a fixed set of vendors whom they had worked with for years. Some of these vendors were also family owned units. The APS owner maintained very good relations with his vendors, some of whom he treated as family.

There were times when vendors would bail out the APS owner, when there was a cash crunch, and vice versa. Mutual support was the binding force between APS and the vendors and this practice went back for quite a few years.

One of APS' key vendors was a fabrication unit. The unit was large and supplied fabricated parts and structures to a number of construction companies. The APS owner's father and the fabrication vendor's father did business together for over 20 years before their sons, the current owners took over. The families knew each other well and the children grew up together.

At this juncture, a new technology with specialized equipment was introduced in the fabrication industry. This technology reduced manufacturing costs by 25%. Many new fabrication vendors who had adopted the new technology started approaching APS to supply their products. They offered products at lower prices and with the same quality. APS and the current fabrication vendor formed a joint team to explore different ways and means to reduce costs and adopt the new technology. The aim of APS was to get supplies at prices that were 15-20% lower. APS was willing to accept a 5% increase over the market price because of the long-standing relationship.

These meetings continued for over six months without any outcome. APS was losing money and their margins were shrinking as they had to align with their competitors. The fabricator however remained adamant and refused to change his manufacturing process to accommodate the new technology. He found some failures of the new technology products in the teething stage and used these to counter the need to adopt the new technology.

Later, when the technology stabilized, he gave reasons that the cost to change was too high, training of workers would be a problem and some may have to be let go. Many of his workers had been with him for 20 years and this could lead to labor problems. Most of all, he felt that at this stage of his life, change would not bring him much joy. The impact on his business would not be that much since 80% of his business was coming from other product lines.

The situation continued for almost two years and the owners got bitter with each other though the families maintained close relationships. APS slowly reduced his business with the vendor and over a period of one year he shifted to another vendor.

The owners of APS and the old fabrication vendor continued to meet in social circles but the bitterness continued. However, they did not allow their disagreements to impact the relations between their families.

In 10 years, the fabricator withdrew slowly and handed his business over to his son. Five years later, the APS owner did the same. The new owners (sons) who had been meeting regularly on the social front slowly gravitated to discussing business which was taboo in the past when their fathers were running the businesses.

Eventually, the younger generation started working together and the retired parents did not restrain them. As a matter of fact, both were happy and soon began encouraging their sons.

Both businesses are now flourishing and there is some talk of setting up a joint venture.

> *Message: Maintaining links while disengaging partnerships is an art that facilitates future reengagement should the need arise. Engagement and disengagement are an important aspect of managing partnerships.*

## Case 3: Managing prioritization with multiple partnerships

A highly talented technologist, John, who had three patents to his name and regularly published 2-3 white papers a year, was well recognized in the engineering industry. He worked for a family owned 'Business Processing Services' (BPS) organization. The BPS division had 15,000 employees and serviced 20 customers. John was the head of the center for technology transformation (CTT) and reported directly to the owner.

The company often acquired business because of their automation and process improvement capabilities which led to cost reduction for their customers. John became a key figure for business acquisition presentations and most of his cost reduction projects were successfully implemented. However, there was a fair degree of dissatisfaction among his colleagues and also his team in the way he treated them. This was because of his 'know-it-all' attitude which put off those that came into contact with him.

The owner appreciated John's contribution and openly praised and supported him against all opposition. Many of the engineers in the project teams who worked on the solutions as well as the operations teams that had to implement the new solutions were unhappy with the treatment, he meted out to them. They felt that their problems and inconveniences were not considered but did not raise the issue as they knew John had the ear of the owner, who was benefitting from the increased business.

After some time, the owner sold the business to a large multinational, which restructured the organization. In the new structure, John was put in a slot which was more than four levels below the CEO. This was because in the new organization, BPS was one of their smaller divisions where the importance given to technology improvements was not a priority.

John left the new company and joined an even bigger multinational that had a 100,000 strong BPS division and was doing over \$4 billion BPS business. They were technology centric and gave their Center for technology transformation (CTT) significant importance. The BPS group had a CEO who had a VP technology under whom three units functioned. The CTT was one of them.

Soon John found out that the VP technology who had 200 people working for him did not have much time for him. He also realized that the VP had a broad spectrum of knowledge but did not have the same level of depth in his area of specialization. The VP expected John to deal directly with the customer relationship managers (CRM) and the 'Business Delivery Managers' (BDM) to sort out problems and move projects forward. John was not used to this as he had always worked under the umbrella of the 'Big Boss' who was the owner in his previous company. He could not get on well with people and often tried to get the VPs support to push operations. When this did not work, he started projecting the VP's incompetence in technology transformation. He then started trying to get the CEO involved.

Whenever there was a crisis in operations, all concerned rallied around John and got their problems solved. However, in 'Business as Usual' (BAU) situations all maintained a good distance from him. At the same time, all acknowledged his superior capabilities.

For three years, the CEO and VP tried to mentor John and to build a bridge between the CRMs and BDMs. Even though there were a few successes, they lasted for a very short span of time.

Many CRMs and BDMs who could not get through to John tried approaching his team members directly. While some team members were receptive to requests made the CRMs and BDMs found that their capability was nowhere close to John's ability to provide solutions. The team members too were unhappy with John.

After five years of significant effort, the management realized that they had a brilliant executive who could solve complex problems but was unable to partner with others in the organization. They also concluded that he was a 'high maintenance' person who was a serious drain on their time and energy. The CEO and VP were 'people persons' but still failed to manage John, who could not partner with others.

Finally, they decided to seclude him from the rest of the organization and only bring him in to solve critical problems. Later the management appointed an external agency to mentor John and help him improve his people skills. This they decided would be the last attempt to resolve the issue.

> *Message: Managing partnership prioritizing is pluralistic and multi-dimensional. Sometimes one comes across brilliant loners who have to be managed. In such cases the compromises and trade-offs made to manage the situation need to be weighed against benefits. There is no straight forward solution for this.*

## Case 4: Effective partnering accelerates progress

A young IT engineer was working in an R&D department of a small multinational company that developed specialized products using state-of-the-art technology. The R&D team were very close, they worked hard, spent nights on the job and celebrated success together. As time went by, these young engineers moved on and one of them, Rene, moved from USA to her home town in Colombo, Sri Lanka (SL).

Back in SL, Rene was offered several jobs but none to her liking. After six months of serious effort, and no luck, she got a call from a colleague in her old company who needed some work done by a person he could trust. Rene had displayed a high degree of integrity while she had worked with the company. The main reason was that besides technical capability, confidentiality was a key factor in the new product development business. Rene was in search of interesting work and at the same time the company wanted a person whom they could trust. This was a perfect match.

Rene accepted the job readily and was well compensated. Soon more work started flowing in. After six months, Rene found it difficult to manage the work alone and needed to get others on board. When she approached her old company, they were not in favor of giving work to an individual who would in turn off-load it to others. It was against company policy. However, the partnership was very strong and Rene helped to pull them out of quite a few crisis situations. They decided to help Rene to set up shop and collaborate with them officially. The board in the USA approved of this route based on Rene's loyalty and trustworthiness. Besides SL was a cost-effective destination for development.

Rene built strong partnerships with those she worked with in the USA and her team in SL learnt to do the same. As a result, there were multi-level partnerships that strengthened the relationship further. In a matter of two years, the company in SL had 500 engineers.

In the next five years, some of her old colleagues moved to other companies and started off loading work to SL. Soon business grew exponentially and Rene who was now middle aged had about 5000 engineers working from three locations in SL.

A deeper look at Rene's journey over 10 years to a 5000-strong company showed that she partnered well with her old colleagues. Being a 'techie', she also managed to cover her low competence areas by partnering with professionals in other functions like administration, finance and marketing. These professionals supported her growth trajectory by doing the work she did not like to do or that she gave a low preference to.

She realized at a young age that partnering is a key to personal and business growth. She also realized that partnering helps to cover lack of knowledge and experience in different fields and functions of business. In short, partnering helps build an holistic and effective team that can deliver desired results.

> *Message: Effective partnering accelerates progress. One cannot be good at everything. It is important to know your strengths and build partnerships in areas where you do not excel. This way you build a tightly integrated holistic team that works to meet client needs.*

## Case 5: Partnerships pay-off in the long run

The Chief Information Officer (CIO) of a large financial institution who had a budget of $3 billion had engaged nine different vendors. He was 30 years into the business and was made the CIO three years before he retired. He had excellent business domain knowledge and constantly updated himself technically.

The CIO managed his vendors very well and put a system in place where he used his vendors to educate his senior staff on technology trends and maintenance techniques. This encouraged the vendors to compete to get a mind share of the CIO in the hope of getting more business. They did this by bringing their R&D heads and leaders of their "Centers of Excellence' to make presentations to the CIOs core team. On the other hand, the vendors benefited as they drew on the CIOs business insights. They used this information to strengthen their strategies and plans. In this manner, the CIO partnered well with the vendors.

Of the nine vendors, five were engaged in development, maintenance and production support in different geographies and business functions. The other four were engaged in separate specialized areas.

While the CIO was firm and tough with the vendors on quality and timely delivery, he was always considerate and made adjustments when they had genuine problems. The vendor execution and customer relationship teams encouraged their CEOs to meet the CIO as he often gave glowing reports of their work. The CEOs were also happy to meet the CIO as he was knowledgeable and shared his insights on the financial sector trends. He was also open to suggestions made by the CEOs on implementation of new technologies and products. In this sense, the CIO built strong partnership relationships with the vendor CEOs.

While the vendors did different work, the CIO engaged with them in a manner that he got the best out of them and, at the same time, satisfied his internal customers. He was able to bring his internal customers and vendors on the same page and resolved several chronic problems that were pain points of the business.

Overall, the CIO's way of dealing with all entities brought about a high level of delivery performance and customer satisfaction.

When the CIO retired, his partnership development capability paid off. He got several offers from vendors to liaise with the company and also with other financial institutions. This made him feel that he had invested his time and effort wisely for the company as well as himself. He, however, only took up one vendor's offer and worked out a consulting arrangement with a few other non-competing vendors.

---

*Message: It is not only important, to engage with clients to get the job done efficiently and effectively, but also to build strong relationships in the process. In this case both the CIO and vendors derived mutual benefit from their engagement. Their sharing of knowledge to help each other, beyond the purpose of their engagement strengthened their partnership bonds. Managing partnerships pays off in the long run.*

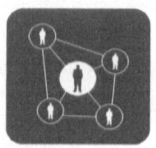

## Chapter 5

# Personal Networking
# A Key Management Capability

### Introduction

Important stakeholders, including senior management executives' network either by design or default. Some are fully aware of networking as an essential part of their job, while many consider it to be 'business as usual' (BAU) with no special emphasis required and yet others are unaware of networking and consider it a social part of their work.

There is no formal acknowledgement of networking as an important capability for senior managers and most learn on their own. As a result, many have wrong perceptions of the why's and how's of networking.

Today networking is a loosely used term and many do not understand what it actually means. Though it is an essential capability for a senior manager to succeed, it is often not considered an important aspect of the job.

To dispel common perceptions, it is important to keep in mind that networking is the process of building relationships for mutual benefit. It is not a 'meet and greet' process carried out at functions to build acquaintances, though this is one way to start the process. However, many people like to think that building acquaintances is what networking is all about.

Networking is important because it helps to enhance awareness in business and professional areas. This could be related to markets, customers, competitors, technologies, regulatory changes and many other areas. It also helps to understand proximity of social, professional and political connections. Depending on the strength of the relationship built, a networking contact could help in providing access to power centers or persons of interest. These connections could be motivated to provide support through their vetoing power besides resource and information sharing.

In the current dynamic and mercenary business environments networking becomes a crucial lever for success. With the current pace of technological innovations, we find customers and competitors are often privy to game changing information on a real time basis. Therefore, in order to stay ahead or even be in the game, it is important to create and maintain personal market intelligence networks. This is besides keeping up with dynamically changing competitor business strategies that directly or indirectly impact your own.

Networking is all about people. Networking experts, those who network to enhance their profession and business goals, assess people before they meet them and decide what they need from these people. This is not all, they also evaluate what they might give in return. This must be something of value to the other person. The bottom line is to appreciate that in networking there are no free lunches. Networking is a 'Give and Take' business.

Networking is also used for building support to create the right image for yourself. People like to work and deal with known people or those they are familiar with. In other words, 'creating the right' image increases the ease of networking. One of the concepts in networking related to image creation is the 'Patron and Champion' concept. A patron is a business leader, politician or senior executive who provides umbrella support for someone below, the champion in this case, to help him achieve his goals. At the same time the champion promotes the patron's image at lower levels to garner support for the patron's endeavors.

At times it is tough to connect with people in senior or influential positions where access is difficult. In such cases it is important to connect with persons below who are more approachable. These people who help build bridges are often one or two levels below. The concept is referred to as 'networking through separation.' Two levels or two degrees of separation is the maximum limit. Networking in cases of separation requires one to manage the needs of the interface person as well as that of the target. This means the 'give and take' relationship would be different for the target and the interface. This makes networking more complex and difficult.

Networking connects are not permanent. As networking is a 'give and take' activity the relationship is based on mutual benefit. When the benefit to any person in the network declines in intensity the connection weakens and the person withdraws. Hence it is important to review the networking circle periodically. Also, networking takes time and effort besides being expensive. It is important to remember that the number of people that can be managed in a network is limited. Hence care must be taken in selecting persons to be included in a network.

At a personal level this is called the 'Circle of Interaction' (COI). The COI in a network keeps changing based on the mutual ability to satisfy needs. This indicates that there would be a throughput of people in a network. Therefore, to manage the network effectively one has to manage the three stages of networking, 'Engage', 'Maintain' and 'Disengage' intelligently. This may not be as easy as it seems and skills need to be developed to handle it well. It is common knowledge that people are always curious as to why someone wants to engage with them or why someone is giving them a cold-shoulder. This is an aspect of managing the 'engage' process. Maintaining relationship interest with periodic 'give and take' swings also requires one to be alert enough to ensure that the right level of interest is retained to sustain the relationship. This is an aspect of managing the 'maintain' process. The 'exit' process also needs to be handled carefully to ensure that goodwill remains even when there is no mutual benefit from engagement.

*Summary: Overall networking is an essential capability for senior stakeholders. It needs to be given the right amount of importance as considerable time, energy and resources are required for it to be effective. Investing in networking is therefore important. This is one of the skill areas where successful people are unaware of the nuances of their own abilities.*

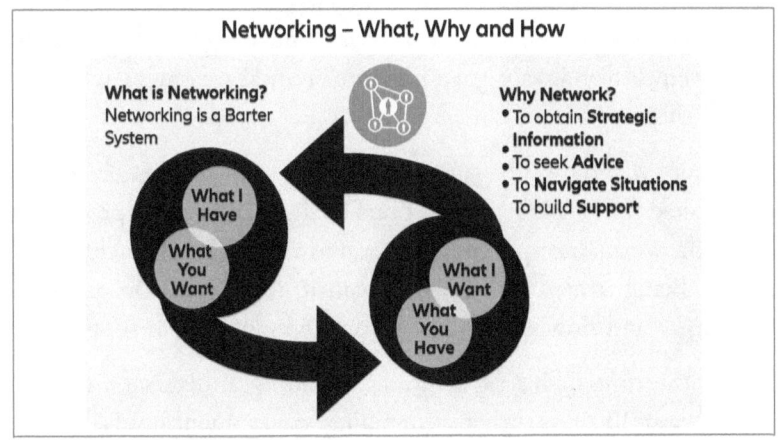

**Networking – What, Why and How**

What is Networking?
Networking is a Barter System

What I Have

What You Want

What I Want

What You Have

Why Network?
* To obtain **Strategic Information**
* To seek **Advice**
* To **Navigate Situations**
To build **Support**

## Personal Networking – A Key Management Capability

## Case Studies

### Case 1: Networking - More than connecting with people

A large multinational conglomerate headquartered in Europe was privately owned. The conglomerate had over 150 operating companies encompassing several primary *business* sectors: chemicals, automotive, hospitality, engineering, consumer products, energy and many others. The conglomerate's assets were about $140 billion and the revenue $130 billion. The number of persons employed by the conglomerate was close to a million.

The personal assistant (PA) to the Chairman of this company was very dynamic and hardworking. He had worked his way up through the ranks and after about 15 years he was selected as PA to the Chairman. While making a number of personal arrangements for the Chairman he got close to the Chairman's friends and family. The Chairman appreciated his work and took good care of him.

He was often asked to meet the heads of government departments, CEO's of the companies in the group and several other business leaders to convey messages from the Chairman. The senior leaders treated the PA well and he got quite friendly with them. They always gave him preferential treatment when he visited them.

Over time, the PA began to build a rapport with the CEOs and often asked for small favors like hotel facilities in five-star properties across the world, transport and sometimes air travel in their chartered planes. Being treated so well, he began to feel he was on par with the CEO's and slowly drew away from some of his old friends.

At the time of his silver jubilee wedding anniversary, the PA invited over 300 guests that were mainly government heads, CEO's and other local dignitaries. Most of them attended. The reception was held in one of the five-star ball rooms and went off very well. He did not invite many of his school friends and others he used to hang out with.

At this stage, the PA felt that the CEOs and other leaders were his circle of interaction (COI). He grew in confidence and started sharing his ideas with them about starting his own small business. They were very encouraging and some even told him that he would be a successful entrepreneur.

In five years, the Chairman retired and a few years later he passed away. The PA who was not doing too well under the new Chairman decided to leave and start his own business. He soon found out that the people who had encouraged him slowly started distancing themselves from him and finally started asking their assistants to meet him. In addition, many of those whom he knew had been transferred or retired.

The PA tried very hard to manage the situation. He went back to his old friends but they too kept their distance. He soon realized that he had lost his old friends and those contacts that he had developed on behalf of the Chairman were only entertaining him because of his relationship with the Chairman. When he got disengaged from the Chairman, they too began to keep him far.

Finally, his business did not take-off and he had to retire. He was financially very well off and money was not a problem as he came from a well to do family. Being the only son, he inherited enough for another generation. However, he was emotionally disturbed as he failed to understand how people had changed.

He eventually realized that networking is more than just connecting with people but also about a mutually beneficial relationship. When the CEOs and government heads found that there was no benefit in keeping the PA in good humor they slowly began to move away.

*Message: Networking is more than just connecting with people – mutual benefit is the key. In this case the PA did not realize that his value in the network was due to his relationship with the Chairman. He also did not maintain links with his old friends to facilitate reengagement in the future. Reciprocity for personal benefit is important for a healthy relationship. When one person is unable to deliver the relationship weakens.*

## Case 2: Managing Social and interlocking networks is complex

A medium sized corporate conglomerate had about 32 companies that were from six different industry sectors with a business of about $25 billion. The Chairman operated on the basis of non-interference. His belief was that as long as the company brought in the mandated profits and worked within the group guidelines there was no need for too much corporate governance. As a result, each company had to fend for itself and deliver results in the open market.

The group was doing fairly well and as per plan when the Chairman retired. The new Chairman was from a financial institution. He had a fairly successful background and was a strong proponent of interlocking directorships. He was in his late 40s and had a strong desire to make a difference and leave a legacy behind. He wanted to take the business to the next level. Besides growing the business, he wanted to double the market capitalization in five to seven years.

One of the novel strategies he used was to adopt social networks and director interlocks with the different group companies and a few other external business houses. He designed a complex system and propagated the concept through his core team.

Within two years he had most of the directors from the boards of the 32 group companies on each other's boards. Some of the directors were also on the boards of select companies outside the group. This way, he built a connect with over a hundred organizations. These connects he put into four categories; companies that would partner for large bids (e.g. hardware and software); companies that could service a wide range of organizations (e.g. transport and travel houses); companies that could work together for mutual benefit (e.g. finance and construction); and Non-Profit organizations to mobilize public support in areas of strategic business goals (charities, foundations, think tanks and R&D Centers)

While individual CEOs that were in touch with each other, appreciated the concept to an extent, very few were privy to the overall big picture game plan. The Chairman however did not interfere in the dealings between organizations but made it clear that the group companies must leverage each other for mutual support.

Initially, there were quite a few misunderstandings as companies had to phase out their old vendors and partners but over time these reduced. Some companies also folded up in the process and a few CEOs preferred to leave the group.

Sometimes, the loss of doing business in the open market was compensated by the comfort of assured business from within the group. Having assured business in the bag, marketing began to concentrate on the outside world and the overall business started to grow. Not only did the bonding between the group of CEOs improve, there was also a lot of cross sharing of market intelligence, technology applications and business trends. By observing the CEO synergies within the group, functional groups started working together at lower levels. Overall, the business grew well. Soon leads for mergers and acquisitions came to light which directly supported the Chairman's market capitalization vision.

The Chairman brought in the networking and interlocking culture subtly. He maintained two degrees of separation between himself and the implementers to ensure that progress was at the pace the group could manage, giving CEOs enough space and time to fall in line.

The group reached $50 billion in revenue and $45 billion in market capitalization in 5 years. All things considered equal, many in the industry were all praise for the Chairman's achievements. However, only a few were able to spot and appreciate the novel networking strategy that he adopted to bring the group closer together and at the same time deliver results above the market norms.

> *Message: Networking is a complex and subtle skill which requires time and patience to develop. In this case the network system designed for overall group engagement was very complex and needed a lot of commitment and drive to implement. However, the subtle management of the Chairman and his confidants, in navigating the implementation, paid off. They ensured that any baggage and agendas of the past were dealt with smoothly.*

## Case 3: More is less in networking

A medium sized automotive OEM subsidiary that was part of a major European group was set up in India to service the Asia Pacific market. In the first five years, the company had some teething troubles that got sorted out by the two successive CEOs sent from their parent company. In the sixth year, when the term of the European CEO was coming to an end, they appointed a senior vice president from one of the Indian companies as CEO. The new CEO came with a good track record and had exceptional management capabilities. He however had the habit of giving his managers a free hand and at the same time he was known for setting challenging targets.

The previous CEOs were hands-on and used to often get into issues that cropped up between the different functional departments.

This kept the balance between the functional heads. The new CEOs management style was different and the functional heads were not used to his hands-off style of management. Soon, there were small squabbles between the different functions at the lower levels. These increased over the months till the animosity and frustration between the functional heads, became glaringly obvious to the CEO. The production head who had become the target of most of the functional heads was on the verge of leaving. This was at a time when one of the old CEOs was visiting the company.

At the behest of the current CEO the visiting CEO did a quick review of the situation across functions and found that:

- Production was having a problem with 'Planning & Scheduling' because of frequent switches in manufacturing schedules which impacted their asset (high value machinery) utilization targets.

- The 'Planning & Scheduling' had a problem with Sales because of their erratic and unplanned orders which continuously disrupted their schedules and brought down their output optimization targets.

- The sales were having a problem with 'Materials and Scheduling' as stocks were not available for immediate supply to preferred customers. This was because of the target on inventory turnover.

- The Maintenance department, was having problems with procurement because of long lead time for critical spares leading to increased machine downtime. Maintenance also needed minimum stock of spares while procurement had pricing targets and needed more lead time for low-cost off-shore procurement

- Logistics had a problem with Sales and Inventory as they had to deliver incomplete orders and partial container load deliveries due to lack of sufficient stocks. Their efficiency and utilization targets were negatively impacted.

Further, there were issues with Finance, Quality, Industrial engineering and R&D.

The old CEO summed up the situation and initially thought that the new CEO was ineffective. However, when he put up his report to the board, they analyzed the situation and found that the first two European CEOs had been selected for their hands-on expertise and they delivered well. However, the current CEO was selected for his capability to grow the business and increase margins through efficiency improvement. To do this, he had to have his functional operations run smoothly and with minimum personal involvement. They also realized that many of the functional heads lacked the maturity to work in an integrated organizational structure. They had performed well when the hands-on CEOs solved their problems.

By this time, the production head had resigned and they selected, Salim, a person with high networking skills who could bring the functional heads together and sort out issues. This meant motivating people to network in order to bring about successful trade-offs and compromises. This approach was acceptable to the CEO who wished to focus on business growth even if it meant making a few compromises.

Salim was network savvy and had studied the organization structure and its integration needs before he joined. He realized that each organization function required a different networking approach to facilitate integration. Salim was aware of his opportunity to contribute and exploited his networking skills to the optimum. One of his successes came from getting functional heads to put up joint proposals of compromises (functional department trade-offs) be made in the overall interest of the company. This brought about a win-win for both parties which in turn led to significant results. He was well appreciated and soon grew to a senior position within the organization.

> *Message: Networking is crucial to success in any role. However, the approach required will vary based on organization structures and interdependencies. This is in addition to stakeholder agendas.*

## Case 4: Networking - A key skill to excel at higher levels

A large government research organization (GRO) in the Asia Pacific region was on the lookout for a mid- level administrative officer to assist them in one of their divisions to execute major projects in specific time frames and budgets. An army colonel who had an outstanding academic career in engineering and who was known for his resolve and grit to meet commitments took early retirement and applied for this position.

He was selected and put onto a $50 million project immediately. He did well and was able to complete the project in record time and created an impression of being a hard task master with high achievement orientation and who was reasonable when situations demanded. In the next few years, his superiors watched him carefully and observed that he had a large network of vendors with whom he maintained good relations and at the same time, demanded that they go the extra mile when the organization needed them to.

He soon moved up the ladder and was shifted from a division administration head to a regional administration head where he had several divisions under his jurisdiction. In this position he had to oversee many projects and quite a few were over a $100 million. He also learnt that he had to work with technical specialists and scientists from different streams who were given contracts to provide innovative solutions for DRO projects.

At this stage, he felt the pressure of dealing with specialists who were leaders in their respective fields. At the same time, he had to interact with vendors who were experts in different engineering streams. They included Chemical, Computer Science, Electrical, Electronics & Communication, Mechanical, Metallurgy, Aeronautics, Civil and others. This was when it dawned on him that his networking skills had been crucial to his past success and if he needed to move forward, he would have to take these skills to the next level.

He soon began to build his own circle of consults in different fields. Sometimes he had two consults in the same field to cross-check advice received in order to ensure that he was on the right path. This helped him to provide the best solutions, keep all stakeholders satisfied and at the same time meet the required deliverable standards.

In 10 years, he reached the top corporate administrative position which reported to the Chairman who was also highly placed in the government hierarchy. At this stage, he had to further sharpen his networking skills. To have more fruitful discussions with the Chairman and get his proposals accepted he found it important to understand the mindset of the Chairman. In order to do this, he studied the backgrounds of the Chairman and his advisors. This knowledge helped him to have a good understanding of the Chairman's thought process. Eventually he was able to align and work well with the Chairman.

When he retired, he had a repository of consultants, professors, practitioners and others whom he used to consult on a regular basis. Looking back, he realized that though he was a good engineer and had exceptional project management skills, networking was the key skill that brought him success. In addition to this, he found that there is no training in this area and that though he was practicing networking at junior levels, he did not differentiate the skill from others. It was midway through his career that it dawned on him to give this skill preferred attention for development.

> *Message: No single person, however brilliant, knows everything, but a group can often be used to fill in the gaps. Networking can build consulting groups to aid people in senior positions and help them excel.*

## Case 5: Networking - A self-taught complex skill

A medium sized automotive ancillary with 5000 employees operated on the outskirts of a 'B' grade city in India. The manufacturing unit was set up in an industrial belt where there were many large major industrial units and their ancillaries. The industrial population was 1.2 million at the time of this experience (mid 80's).

In one of the production lines of the automotive ancillary, there was a fairly average junior manager, Robin, with good people skills. Robin was a native of a nearby village. After completing his diploma in mechanical engineering, he joined this ancillary as a trainee supervisor. After a probationary period of six months he was confirmed as a junior supervisor. He did well and in the first six years he received two promotions to the current junior management position. While Robin was well respected by his colleagues and bosses, he was restless and did not see much future in his career. This was because most of his seniors were just a few years older than him and the opportunities were not many. He also had some constraints of leaving the current location of work because of his aged parents and their family business in the village. He was well liked in the community and was a very helpful person by nature.

One day there was a major event held by the Life Insurance Corporation of India (LIC) in the area. The aim was to boost sales and recruit new agents. Existing managers and agents were asked to bring their friends along. Robin accompanied one of his friends to the event. The Regional manager of LIC, a charismatic and dynamic person made an impactful presentation. During the tea break, Robin was introduced to the regional manager by his friend. They immediately struck up a relationship and Robin registered as an agent. He was about 30 years old at this point of time.

Robin who continued working in the auto-ancillary initially sold policies to his friends and relatives. He then moved on to motivate a few colleagues to buy policies. One day, when a new senior manager joined the company as his boss, Robin realized that the new manager was struggling to get settled. He had trouble to get his children into school, his gas connection transferred, his ration card registered and many other small but irritating issues. Robin, who knew most people in the locality decided to help him. Very soon Robin realized that this way of assisting others brought him closer to people. Also, people started buying policies because of his helpful nature. The senior manager who did not believe in LIC policies took a small LIC policy just because of his relationship with Robin.

As Robin realized the impact of his ability to assist people, he started helping all new managers joining the ancillary. The HR department started directing people to him and encouraged him to help new managers settle down. In a few years, he became the go-to guy for getting things done. Soon this spread to other companies in the industrial belt and he started getting many customers referred to him. He then set up a small team to assist in the paperwork and logistics. He however maintained the personal touch. His image grew in LIC and he became a model agent touching Rs 10 million ($400,000 at that point of time) in annual sales, within seven years. His instrumental relationships with different agencies/organizations (Gas, ration, schools etc.) helped him to connect with people and get things done for everyone's mutual benefit. Robin, a junior manager cum LIC agent did well and retired as comfortably as many of his seniors.

His senior manager, Raghu, who was keenly watching Robin's growth, studied his success levers and tried to replicate Robin's model in his own sphere of work. He had limited success initially and found that information brokering was not enough to build successful and mutually beneficial networks. The currency of exchange was important. The value also decided the degree of reciprocation by connected parties to a great extent.

Raghu started identifying a circle of interaction required to meet his near and medium-term objectives and worked on building a mutually beneficial relationship with each entity in the circle. This was because each had a different need. The mutual support helped to overcome the operation gaps and overlaps in the functioning of the company. This was especially where there were cross functional processes. Raghu soon became a popular figure because of his relationships and networking ability. This was over and above his other engineering and management skills, which were also excellent. Raghu was promoted as general manager of the plant and later retired as the vice president of operations.

After retiring, Raghu reflected on his career growth path and tried to identify the levers that had led to his success and also if there were any drawbacks. He found that he intuitively had been using four levers of networking with some variations. They were Support: The ability to develop and to make arrangements for providing mutual support at committee and board meetings. This was also applied to projects (mergers and acquisitions or expansions, etc.) that each stakeholder took up. Access: Providing each other access to people of influence or to data that helped to form strategy or take decisions. Resources: Sharing or providing resources to each other. These included consultants, experts, plant and machinery, etc. Information: Sharing timely information on market trends, government policies, competitor plans besides market intelligence and strategies.

Raghu, however, also realized that he had not spent much effort on personal image management which would have enhanced his career growth. There were two aspects he identified: One was to build a group of Patrons who would provide him an umbrella to act more freely and promote his image at higher levels and among more influential people. The second was that he could have nurtured more champions who would advocate his plans and strategies at the operational level thus making execution more acceptable and effective. Champions would also help to promote his image at the operational level.

He felt that if he had worked on these aspects he could have done better in his career. He, however, realized that the networking game would have become more complex and difficult. It was a question as to whether he could manage the degree of difficulty and complexity. He concluded that he had done a good job and felt happy and satisfied with his achievements.

*Message: Networking is a complex skill and it is mostly self-taught on the job. Robin used the company as a platform to grow his LIC business. Being of service to the company that employed him was an advantage. Raghu used networking to grow in his career. Both Robin and Raghu used networking to achieve higher levels of success and at the same time ensured benefit to the company they worked for.*

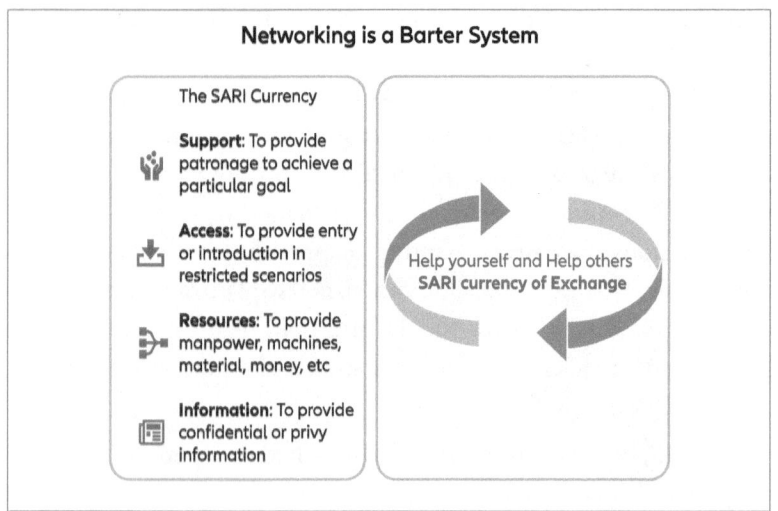

**Networking is a Barter System**

The SARI Currency

**Support:** To provide patronage to achieve a particular goal

**Access:** To provide entry or introduction in restricted scenarios

**Resources:** To provide manpower, machines, material, money, etc

**Information:** To provide confidential or privy information

Help yourself and Help others
SARI currency of Exchange

Chapter 6

# Managing Intra-Organizational, Cross-Border Conflicts

## Introduction

The concept of this chapter on intra-organizational, cross-border conflicts has been developed in the backdrop of the corporate world. The practical issues that come up between departments, divisions, subsidiaries, franchises, partners and others are many. While there are policies in place to facilitate the overall functioning of an organization, grey area management of cross-border conflicts is not given much conscious attention. While this discussion is limited to corporates, the frame of reference for cross-border conflicts could also apply to other types of institutions such as non-governmental and non-profit organizations.

The general thinking is that if an organization has strong policies and systems in place, it can achieve a high level of excellence. However, in practice much time and effort of senior management is spent on effective management of grey areas and political dynamics.

A point to note is that there are no thumb rules for managing informal structures that surpass boundaries and have a very real influence on the outcomes of organizations.

A true-life example that could be used to support the intra-organizational conflict concept would be the case of Sony. The analysis of published reports on the Sony case brings out nearly all the facets related to issues in intra-organizational, cross-border conflicts. Political rivalry between powerful divisions in the company was the major cause of its downfall. The fall of Sony was because of the disastrous infighting between its hardware and software streams. The mismanagement of this rift led to strategic moves in the wrong direction, that is, supporting hardware over software and the internet. The inability to manage border encroachment for the overall benefit of the company proved to be their downfall. Some extracts from analysts' reports are given below:

## Reports

- New York Times: How the Tech Parade Passed Sony By - Hiroko Tabuchi https://www.nytimes.com/2012/04/15/technology/how-sony-fell-behind-in-the-tech-parade.html

- Gizmodo: How It All Went Wrong For Sony - Jamie Condliffe https://.com/5902234/how-it-all-went-wrong-for-sony

- HBR: Strategy, Context, and the Decline of Sony - Sohrab Vossoughi https://hbr.org/2012/04/strategy-context-and-the-decli

## Extracts

- Though Akio Morita, the co-founder of Sony Corp. knew the right thing to do he was unable to get the warring teams to follow.

- Leaders had trouble wielding authority over the sprawling company. Sony remains dominated by proud, territorial engineers who often shun cooperation.

- What went wrong is a tale of lost opportunities and disastrous infighting. It is also the story of a proud company that was unwilling or unable to adapt to realities of the global marketplace. An example is the MP3 player: Sony had the technological and musical background to launch an iPod-beating digital music device long before Apple launched its device. It never happened.

- Sony made three big mistakes: It focused on releasing cutting-edge hardware at the expense of releasing products on time and creating software; its catalogue products became bloated and confusing; and its on line strategy sucked.

Most organizations set up strong policies, systems and processes, in order to encourage empowerment and ownership to manage routine and day-to-day operations more efficiently. These indirectly inculcate a silo attitude in departments for purposes of efficiency and focused target achievement. While this is good to an extent, it is not possible for an organization to operate in watertight compartments. This is especially so when an organization has to be innovative and remain competitive in order to achieve higher level goals. Market dominance or brand leadership comes from being flexible, agile and highly responsive to market dynamics. In the case of Sony, it was a question of being able to ride the technology wave. Sony hardware and software divisions operated as separate empires at the cost of the overall benefit of the organization.

In most corporations, the intertwining and integration of functional operations is the key to success. The problem is that, at different levels, it often becomes difficult to determine where ownership begins and ends. Often, the problem starts when people are passionate about an idea and believe it to be beneficial for the department or organization without the full knowledge of the overall dynamics of the situation. For example, some situations could be caused by a brilliant idea that:

- Is not in line with the overall organization strategy;

- Involves a tremendous skill change among staff that are happy with the status quo;

- Causes resistance to change because of increased workload or no benefits to those affected;

- Instigates individual egos and personal rivalry especially among powerful entities; or

- Causes a change in the power dynamics of the different entities in the organization.

The ability to manage the affected entities including the idea generator is difficult. The issue is often very complex.

Managing grey areas and political dynamics requires more than just a rational approach at all levels of the hierarchy. In today's world, the selection of high-level professionals are based on their intelligence quotient (IQ) and emotional quotient (EQ) besides knowledge gained from relevant experience.

To manage ownership at any level and to cut across organizational boundaries for success, a leader should normally have:

- A broad overview of complementary functional disciplines;

- A good level of trust and relationships with others where border grey areas exist;

- A clear picture of the overall organizational goals;

- Respect for the expertise and judgement of others in specialized fields; and

- A fair and realistic assessment of the overall situation (internal and external).

All this needs to be taken into consideration with the organization change capability index. In addition, the attitude of the hierarchy involved, which could range from conservative to adventurous, needs to be factored in while taking any decision.

While managing these conflicts may be very simply orchestrated, in actual practice, it is a stupendous task. The art of managing intra-organizational, cross-border conflicts can only be developed from 'reflective experiential learning'. Text book and class room education helps but experience with conscious learning is the key.

*Summary: Managing intra-organizational cross border conflicts requires more than just a rational approach. Appreciation of the context and political dynamics is also important. In the Sony case the CEO knew the right thing to do but was unable to execute. This was because the political resistance was too strong and the time was short.*

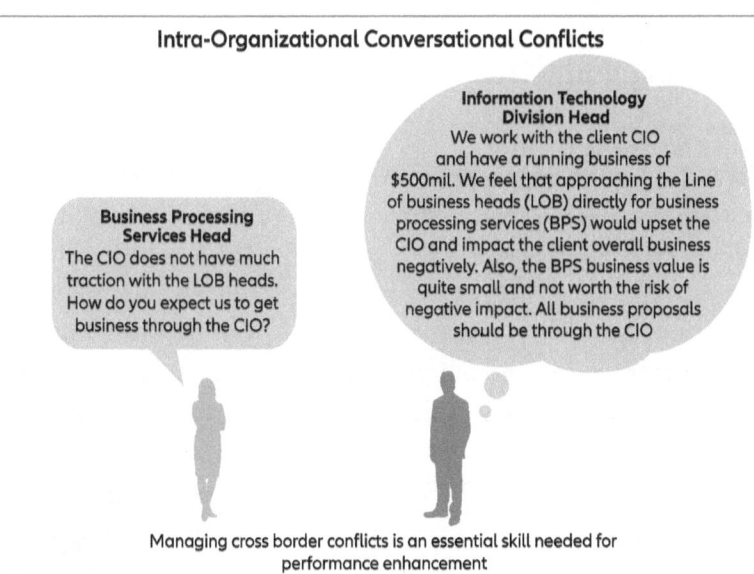

**Intra-Organizational Conversational Conflicts**

**Information Technology Division Head**
We work with the client CIO and have a running business of $500mil. We feel that approaching the Line of business heads (LOB) directly for business processing services (BPS) would upset the CIO and impact the client overall business negatively. Also, the BPS business value is quite small and not worth the risk of negative impact. All business proposals should be through the CIO

**Business Processing Services Head**
The CIO does not have much traction with the LOB heads. How do you expect us to get business through the CIO?

Managing cross border conflicts is an essential skill needed for performance enhancement

## Managing 'Intra–Organizational' 'Cross-Border' Conflicts

## Case Studies

### Case 1: Ego management and informal structures

A large engineering consultancy company having over 200,000 employees across the world had a dynamic CEO who was able to get the best out of his people. In trying to understand the secret of his success a few young managers (MBAs) started studying his management style. The objective was not only to find out what made him tick but also to pick up some tools and techniques for their own personal development.

After observing the CEO for a period of three months one of the things they came across was that though the organization chart showed 35 people reporting to the CEO there were over a 100 who claimed they were reporting to him. On further investigation they found that most of the people who claimed to be reporting to the CEO were high profile experts in their fields and though they were shown as reporting to the different divisional heads they were frequently in touch with the CEO.

The organization structure was designed along industry sectors. Business divisions included banking, Insurance, Utilities, Power and Automobile besides others. While Sector specific business catered to client needs in a focused manner the company also had several technology centric units that provided support across businesses.

The business divisions were responsible for revenue and the VPs heading the businesses were powerful people as each of them was responsible for bringing in considerable revenue. The business heads and the CEO worked as a close-knit team. However, the Technology heads provided the cutting-edge technology that helped in business acquisition. They were high profile people known in the industry and were often called upon by the business heads to showcase innovative solutions to clients. These technology experts were recognized internationally and were sought after by the competition.

The CEO realized that he had to keep the technology heads happy by managing their egos. He did this by giving them the right amount of attention; guiding them on how best to promote their image at different platforms and encouraging them to come out with white papers and patents. To do this, he had frequent discussions with them bypassing their direct bosses who were the divisional heads. This informal structure worked well to balance the management of both the business and technology heads.

The CEO however had to spend long hours to manage such a large number of formal and informal leaders in the organization. These interactions gave the CEO much knowledge of the latest technology trends which he incorporated in his talks and press conferences, there by projecting himself as a forward-looking leader.

The CEO managed intra-organizational cross border communication well without letting others feel that he was intruding. Even divisional heads, whom the technology experts reported to, were happy with the informal system as it relieved them of the task to manage such high-profile personalities with large egos and dogmatic views.

The young managers who were studying the CEO got a good understanding of the way in which the CEO was working with different leaders in the organization. However, they were not able to visualize the gamut of competencies required to manage these cross-border relationships.

After a few years when the CEO moved on to become the Chairman of another group, the next incumbent found it difficult to manage this formal and informal structure. After struggling for some time, he restructured the organization making all technology heads report to a single executive vice president. While this looked good on paper he realized his mistake when a few key technology experts resigned.

It was then that the young managers realized that the art of managing cross border communication successfully is an art that can only be mastered through conscious experiential learning.

---

*Message: Intra organizational conflicts are not only related to differences in business development and execution issues. In this case, it was the ego management of major contributors who promoted business indirectly. The CEO used informal structures to keep all the stake holders happy and also by meeting the diverse needs of the experts.*

---

## Case 2: Managing results across divisions with conflicting policies

As with most corporate, the Armed Forces also have their fair share of Intra organizational cross border conflicts. Though there are strong systems and a high level of discipline, those in higher command positions still need to have the skills and maturity to manage cross border conflicts.

In one of the Corps Head Quarters (*Corps is a main subdivision of an army in the field, under it are divisions and brigades*), of a medium sized army in the 80's, a new General Officer Commanding (GOC) took over charge. He was a very ambitious and result oriented person. Among several priority tasks before him, the one that got him worrying was, that the overall communication in the Corps zone was not satisfactory. Inadequate communication facilities were making it difficult for commanders to function and be in close touch with their subordinate troops in border outposts. He asked the officer representing the communication branch to make a presentation to understand the complexity and scope of the problem. The root cause identified was that though the equipment supplied to the Corps was as per the authorized type and scale, the configuration was not adequate to meet the current needs. Also, over time some of the equipment was out dated. This disturbed the GOC and he took it up with seniors at the headquarters. However, he got into a lot of red tape and nothing moved for a year.

In the meantime, a new communication branch head (CBH) was posted in and the GOC took out his frustrations on him. Not knowing the full situation, the new CBH asked for a month's time to study the situation and come back with a plan. The GOC grudgingly agreed though he felt nothing worthwhile would come out.

The new CBH took the assignment seriously and travelled to all formations in the Corps Zone, interacted with commanders and other end users at various levels, obtained feedback and suggestions from commanding officers of communication battalions and visited 20 odd outposts. At times he had to walk for almost a day to reach an outpost. However, he met the troops in most difficult locations and got a firsthand view of things.

Now the problem was to come up with a plan. As there were many tasks to be taken up, the CBH prioritized them in three categories of which the highest priority was for communication to the border outposts. He developed a project plan in a manner that tasks could be taken up in parallel and at the same time in order of priority. He also realized that while some tasks could be done within the available resources, there were quite a few that required support from the Central HQ to get the new and additional equipment released. The high priority tasks identified by him involved relocation of some of the existing resources as also induction of new and latest equipment. The limitation was that the transmission equipment procured five years ago and provided to outposts had limited range and this made it difficult for the junior commanders and their seniors to communicate among themselves as the geographical locations had extended over a period of time. Though the equipment in use was approved by the commanders five years ago, it did not meet the operational needs of the present. He realized that putting across this point to the GOC would not only make him furious but it would also not offer any solution. The CBH then made a detailed presentation to the GOC to explain to him his approach to the solution. This involved highlighting priorities, relocation of the existing equipment, additional resources needed besides others. The GOC was impressed with the presentation and suggested a few changes. He however, made it clear that he wanted to see the results within six months. This was especially in resolving communication issues related to border outposts. He also promised to take up cases with the Central HQ. This forged the beginning of a relationship of respect and trust between the GOC and the CBH.

This change of heart of the GOC enthused the CBH. He took up the matter with communication branch bosses departmentally. He and his representatives also obtained availability status of suitable equipment from the Army depots and some that were under trial with users outside the Corps zone. He visited some depots and locations to observe the equipment under trial.

On inspection of the available equipment, he selected those that could be directly used and others that could be used after some modifications. He then went to the GOC and sought his intervention to procure the equipment. This approach worked and after some persuasion, the Central HQ agreed to release the necessary equipment in a phased manner over next six months. As this schedule was not appealing to the GOC, he asked his senior in the hierarchy to intervene to speed up the release. The GOC even spoke to the Vice Chief of the Army and with their joint effort; the entire equipment was released on high priority.

The equipment was received in two months and was installed with much effort in a record time of three months. Finally, the GOC was able to talk to his outposts nine months after the CBH took over the new position.

This example shows that willingness to work across boundaries in search of solutions can bring unbelievable results. The CBH was willing to explore solutions instead of quoting policies, rules and past histories. The GOC was able to see talent and tenacity in the CBH. They worked as partners to find a workable solution. The CBH was rewarded handsomely for his achievements and became known for his ability to work across boundaries to deliver results.

Intra organizational cross border conflict resolution starts with building respect and trust. This is besides the willingness to push boundaries, use contacts and explore solution opportunities. Sticking to standard policies and practices which are good for routine activities generally lead to blocks in complex and uncommon situations.

*Message: Building relationships and trust play an important role in resolving intra organizational conflict. In situations where there is a trust deficit because of past experiences, it takes more time and effort to normalize before moving forward. This must be taken into consideration when working towards a resolution.*

## Case 3: Managing power centers and resistance to change

A large transnational organization had many divisions that manufactured and sold different products. These divisions came into being because of the aggressive organic growth strategy that one of the earlier Chairmen had followed. One such division that was set up was for switch gear products to be supplied to the power sector.

The division grew well for the first 10 years and captured a major share of the domestic market. Looking to expand, the CEO mandated the sales to explore the possibility of exporting the products. He also fixed modest targets for exports in the first year.

The sales team went all out to meet the new targets and made a few sales at marginal profits. They soon learnt that competitor products were of a slightly better quality and had additional features. Bringing this feedback to their R&D department, the sales VP initiated a project to find out how the current product could be modified to compete in the international markets.

They soon found out that with some modifications in the die-casting and machining processes the product could be made competitive in the international market. The VP then took up the issue with the CEO who asked the industrial engineering and methods department to work out the changes required in the production equipment and related processes. This was to be worked out along with the cost effectiveness of the whole proposal.

The final report presented to the CEO was encouraging and the ROI was attractive. The CEO gave the go-ahead to introduce the changes in the product design and manufacturing processes.

When this came to the production department the project team met with immense resistance. Most of the workers and managers had moved from other divisions to the switch gear division and had to reorient themselves to new production skills. They had been chosen because of their superior experience and because it was a chance for career growth. However, the new proposal was perceived as an inconvenience with no benefit to the workers and managers. They began finding fault in the methods suggested and raised numerous practical difficulties. The workers and managers who were originally transferred to the division were at their prime but now most of them had crossed 50 and were looking for a smooth tenure without any stress till they retire.

The resistance was brought to the notice of the CEO who did not want to rock the boat as business was good in the current state. It was a sellers' market for the company and the production department was a major player to bring in profits. The production managers over the years continuously came up with innovative methods to increase production. They were able to achieve a target of 30% above the desired capacity. This made production a favorite of the CEO. Their outstanding performance helped him to get a lot of kudos at the shareholder AGMs over the years.

The CEO tried to convince the production team but was not able to get them to agree. While the new modified product was a good initiative for the long run it was clear that the plan for the next 3-4 years could be easily achieved with the current setup. He therefore decided to put off the decision of modifying the product and process. This was a boost to the production department who extended themselves to perform better through cost cutting and production enhancement initiatives. Slowly the new project went into the background and was not taken up strongly again.

The CEO moved on to another larger division and the new modified product went into cold storage. After about seven years the company started losing market share and decided to revamp their product. By this time the competitors had upgraded their products and foreign products had also entered the local market. The company tried to retrieve the situation but the performance moved downwards.

Finally, after another three years the company hived off the division to a competitor as running a division with an outdated product was no longer feasible.

Managing intra organizational cross border conflicts is an art where managing culture and attitude plays an important role. Resistance to change is often the most difficult aspect to tackle when introducing new initiatives especially if it affects personal agendas. Top management often needs to look at trade-offs between business growth and cross border issues.

> *Message: Managing intra organizational conflicts often comes down to personal agendas and resistance to change. Very often stakeholders carry baggage and do not wish to change for genuine personal reasons. In this case the CEO could have tried harder to work out compromises and trade-offs for long term organizational benefit.*

## Case 4: Balancing the human and business elements in conflicts

A major European conglomerate had established a subsidiary in India which was doing very well. The Asia Pacific region head was so impressed with the sales team of the Indian subsidiary that she visited India to see for herself how the team had surpassed all expectations.

During her visit she was very impressed with the working style and the customer connects. She however noticed that the information technology (IT) systems were archaic especially in the sales division. To raise the level of performance and also as a gesture of goodwill, she sent the corporate office IT team to do a study and come up with a solution to improve the sales management system. She also made it clear that budget for the new system would not be a problem and that they should go in for a state-of-the-art system with all the bells and whistles.

A team of experienced IT professionals came to India and conducted a study. They did a thorough needs analysis in which the sales team participated whole heartedly. The local Indian IT team were also on board and supported the approach being taken. On completion of the study, the report was sent to the India head (CEO) who approved of the recommendations. He was close to the sales team as much of the credit that the Indian subsidiary received was because of their performance. To make sure that all entities were committed to the project the CEO called a meeting between the local IT, the corporate IT, the sales team and also the other departments like finance and inventory. All unanimously agreed to support the initiative.

In a bid to move fast the CEO asked the local IT group to put out requests for proposals (RFPs) to reputed vendors and fixed a time frame of two months by which time the project should kick-off.

All went well and one of the top three vendors with a track record of developing sales systems worldwide was selected. The project was awarded and the work started on time. However, the system that was promised in 18 months took three years because of several delays in client (sales team) acceptance and testing procedures. Also, the sales team kept making many changes and often reversed their decisions. There seemed to be varying views on user friendliness among the sales team members. This was mostly because many of the sales team members were not tech-savvy.

After many minor modifications the sales team accepted the system. However, at the time to go live the project got stuck. There were several training programs and hand holding strategies adopted to help the sales team use the system but to no avail. After a year of seriously trying the vendor withdrew and the local IT group too gave up. The CEO was concerned as much money was spent on the system and the global corporate management were keen to see the benefits. He mandated an intervention by the HR department who in turn hired a vendor that specialized in organizational development interventions. He also asked them to put a change management consultant on the intervention team.

After three months of focused group meetings and personal interviews the consultants came to the conclusion that the sales head and his senior colleagues were around 50 years of age. The sales heads had initially agreed to the project and only went along to keep the global corporate management happy. They were not aware of what the sales system would entail when they took the decision to go ahead. They felt uneasy with the degree of transparency that the new system provided to the higher management. During the study phase they put a team of youngsters to interact with the IT professionals. Based on the inputs from the young professionals, the sales heads approved the designs without knowing their full implications.

On receiving the consultant's report from the HR department, the CEO realized he was in a catch-22 situation. The global corporate management were demanding implementation and the sales heads, who were the backbone of the local operation were reluctant to take the implementation seriously. It was found that the corporate IT team that conducted the study and put up the proposal had not taken into consideration the behavioral patterns of the users. Hence, they did not anticipate any resistance to change.

The CEO assessed the current situation and felt that the whole organization was tense as the global corporate management was watching the developments closely. The sales heads' resistance to the new sales system was not expected nor were any signals of resistance detected. They were a powerful partner in the local subsidiary's success story. He concluded that this was not a time to play the blame game or take a tough stand with the sales heads.

When the CEO reviewed the problem with his mentor, they came to the conclusion that all concerned did not pick up any behavioral signals that indicated future implementation resistance. The second point was that the sales management team was a powerful lobby and the prime contributor to the organization and their high-performance level.

Considering all options, the CEO decided that rocking the boat was not the answer as achieving business targets were his main objective. He decided to use the system partially (less than 25% of its full potential) with the younger sales staff and plan for a complete implementation in 3-5 years. He convinced global corporate management to overlook the intra-organizational conflict and allow the sales to continue functioning like they did before. This would release the tension in the subsidiary and business growth would not be affected.

Managing intra-organizational conflict is an art that requires a high amount of emotional intelligence to understand and appreciate the behavioral patterns and relationships across stake holders. The problem had occurred because of overlooking the human angle in implementing a change. The solution was based on releasing the organizational tension (emotional situation) to enable better focus on business. The situation was handled in a damage control manner, the scars however would take time to heal.

> Message: Managing intra organizational conflicts often boils down to appreciation of the human angle while implementing change. In this case the CEO delayed implementation so as not to affect the morale of major business contributors. At the same time, he gave them the time and space to align with the change required.

## Case 5: Managing border encroachment and political agendas

One of the top 10 global financial institutions had set up a subsidiary in India. The structure of the organization was such that the business verticals reported to the respective business heads at the headquarters. They were also required to report locally to the country head who was responsible for the smooth functioning of the local operations.

The subsidiary had been in operation for over 25 years and were well adapted to the local market. Business was good and growth as per the planned strategy was conservative. In one of their business streams a new MD joined. He was young and aggressive and soon got down to understanding the business. In the first year he re-aligned the structure and operations of the sales teams to enable a more aggressive market outreach. Though the targets were exceeded marginally, a strong platform for future growth had been put in place. In the second year he pushed for higher targets and achieved a 35% growth, something that was not seen in the subsidiary for many years and also not common in the parent organization. This brought him good visibility and also raised the expectations of his global bosses. However, the country head who was slightly conservative by nature was uncomfortable with the situation for two reasons; first, the MD was getting too much visibility for his liking and the second was that he felt that this growth trajectory was not sustainable. He felt that in future he would be asked awkward questions if the growth dropped.

The new MD realized that he would have to offer new products to sustain this growth rate.

The next year the MD rode the success wave but at the same time found that a product being offered in more matured markets could be introduced locally with a bit of tweaking. He got his team to study the product and investigate the market needs so that the product could be customized to meet the local market demands. The next step was to get the legal group to vet the product to meet local regulatory conditions. This was a major task as the local laws were quite different and any changes would have a ripple effect on other conditions. However, after several iterations and reviews by external consultants the product was good to go.

At this stage the local country head who was cynically watching the progress and did not expect this initiative to go through, stepped in. Though he did not have any jurisdiction on the business stream, he put up a case to the top management that the proposal was too risky and there were possibilities of getting into legal tangles.

The MD and his team had several meetings with the country head but could not come to any agreement. The bottom line was that besides a personality clash the country head kept harping on some imaginary risks which even the legal experts felt were too farfetched. The MD then took the matter up with the business stream board who after assessing the case objectively supported the MD as the business projections outweighed the risks. The MD got the go ahead.

The high visibility of the case put the pressure on the MD to perform. By this time his team was charged. They took ownership of the product as they were involved in the design from the beginning. In the 4th year the MD and his team achieved a growth of 50% which was a record in the history of the financial institution worldwide.

The intra organizational border conflict in this case, while resolved at a higher level, left much bad blood between the MD and the country head. This could have been resolved by better relationship management of all stakeholders. Better engagement between the Country Head and the MD from the inception of the new product strategy would have helped to some extent considering the uncomfortable relationship between the two.

Managing intra organizational border conflicts not only depends on the issue itself but also on the relationship history of those involved. The art is in knowing this and managing the situation in a reasonable timeframe with least frictional losses.

> *Message: Intra organizational conflict when managed through a third party often leaves scars. This is especially so in a win-lose situation. A better approach would be to anticipate the resistance and work towards a mutually agreeable solution in advance. Only if this fails the escalation route should be followed.*

## Case 6: Cross border collusion and camouflaging of faults

A large transnational organization in the energy sector business had a subsidiary that was doing well in a developing country. In addition to supplying state of the art equipment to the local market they were able to manage exports to account for 40% of their business. Most export was to Europe and some to countries in the Asia Pacific region. Though the pricing was competitive the margins were high because of the lower labor costs.

The subsidiary was doing well and had been in business for the past 15 years. It was at this stage that the CEO who had been with the company for the past 10 years left to join another multi-national that was in the same line of business.

The head office decided to hire a new CEO who was young with a track record of looking at things differently and with a creative bent of mind to improve productivity. They believed the marketing function was doing well and that it was time to consolidate and improve the operations.

The new CEO, Kumar, was very professional in his approach. He was tech-savvy and had a track record of creative improvements for higher efficiency with an acumen for managing resistance to change. He also was in the habit of getting to the root cause of a problem fairly quickly.

On joining Kumar set himself a target of three months to get himself familiarized with the different operations of the company. During this period, he noticed that quite a few of the existing processes had flaws which were being camouflaged in reporting.

On the completion of three months he initiated a process management audit. The audit report highlighted that there were quite a few small parts being purchased that could not be traced to the equipment being sold. While the total amount involved was not very high he was intrigued to find out the reason. On further investigation he found out that about 20% of the orders were being shipped to customers without some small parts. In return customers withheld 10% of the payment as per the short supply clause in the contract. This left a number of invoices pending closure for want of parts supply.

What Kumar found was that over time, a number of invoices were closed at the company end with small amounts written off. This was deemed OK as margins were high. But what was more surprising was that the sales maintained dual records of invoices pending closure. One was on the system that was visible to the headquarters and the other manually maintained by the sales team. At a point of time the system showed 30 pending invoices and the manual record had 90 cases pending.

The CEO then began to look into the issue and found that many departments were responsible for this situation. The reasons they gave were:

- Production – Need to ship equipment before the month end to meet delivery targets
- Purchase – Unable to get parts on time due to last minute changes in customer specification
- Design – Last minute changes in customer requirements
- Sales – Customer comes first –unable to control customer changes or extended delivery schedule
- Inventory – Parts found missing at the last moment before shipping
- Quality Control – Functional inspection was OK by customer inspectors and QA. Accessories were to be fitted at customer site later.

He found that all departments knew about this and were comfortable with the way things worked. Everyone remained quiet as there was a cover-up of each other's short comings and the old CEO knew of this too. The headquarters were happy as the overall profitability and growth figures looked good. Most years the target was exceeded. It was like a happy boys' school. All's well that ends well.

On scrutinizing the backlog of unclosed invoices, he found that some of them were pending for over five years. He felt that the situation would blowup sooner or later and a lot of mud-slinging would take place. He also felt that if he did not tackle the situation now, he would become part of it. However, being new he did not want to rock the boat too much. Taking a tough stand to clean up the mess would leave scars on many local managers as well as those in the headquarters. Also over the years the head office auditors had not found any discrepancies during their yearly reviews.

He decided to tackle the problem differently. He called a meeting of all the department heads and asked them to nominate young managers from each of their departments to form a 'task force' for the cleanup. He gave the task force one week to come up with a plan and three months to clear the backlog. He also monitored progress personally on a weekly basis.

In three months 90% of the backlog was cleared and the rest in the next three months. The process was tightened up and things improved drastically.

Intra organizational conflicts across boundaries if not managed properly can lead to an unholy union of stakeholders that work against the interests of the company at large. At times deploying people without baggage and with fresh and innovative minds can help solve problems with past histories. Managing collaboration across boundaries in the midst of conflict is an art not easily learnt. Conscious experiential learning is key to one's personal development at the higher rungs of management.

> *Message: The art of managing intra organizational conflict is complex. Managing to ensure a 'face-saving' scenario is part of that art. Conscious experiential self-learning is key to development of this art.*

Conclusion

# Putting it Together
# Points of Action

This book is primarily for top performers at senior levels who wish to become more successful. The aim is to facilitate the desire to excel further or aid the successful to reach their full potential. The focus is to provide thought triggers to enable better conscious experiential learning through satellite and diverse sources.

## Achieving a Level of Success

The three factors that contribute considerably to achieve a high level of personal success are:

- **Environmental Dynamics:** Environmental dynamics are governed by situation-influencing factors which are under continuous change. Some such factors would be customer trends, competition, innovation, regulations, natural disasters or wars and political or economic change. This leads to the universal truth that:

  - To be good one must follow proven tracks. The problem with this approach is that new environmental elements, which might impact the situation, are not given due consideration. Hence optimal results may not be achieved.

- To be great one needs to carve one's own path. This ensures current environmental elements are integrated with the wisdom of the past to provide a holistic and optimal solution.

Hence the title: Carve your own path to success

- **Grey Area Management:** It is common knowledge that the need to manage grey areas keeps on increasing for a manager on the path to the top. The ambiguity at the top grows and decision-making based on assumptions becomes a way of life. Growth transition stages move from following instructions at lower levels to following processes at middle levels to making promises based on assumptions at higher levels. Making good decisions at senior levels requires more and more knowledge and information in diverse areas. The number of unknowns also builds up substantially.

Grey area management is also connected with stress. Higher stress levels at senior positions require enhanced stress management skills. This is often not a consideration by the appointed or the appointer.

- **Conscious Experiential Learning:** Success comes from continuous and conscious experiential learning. The myth is that if you work in a particular area for 20 years you have 20 years' experience and therefore you have that much knowledge – but it could well be 20 years of doing routine, repetitive work with very little knowledge acquisition. This is the reason why we see managers with the same life-time experience having a wide difference in their level of capability. Knowledge acquisition is based on a persons' ability to consciously learn while working. The ability to pick up multidimensional and diverse insights from a work situation, at any point of time, is the key to enhancing knowledge levels. An example to depict the point:

The business development head of a unit visited a client with a proposal. He took along with him the local sales manager and a subject matter expert. The unit head who they reported to met all three of them separately to find out how the meeting went. Their responses:

- Sales Manager: I did not get enough time to share my thoughts related to the practical aspects of the proposed solution. This would have helped in convincing the client.

- Subject Matter Expert: I explained the solution well and the client accepted our point of view. He was convinced with our proposal.

- Head – Business Development: The client was OK but they have not budgeted for a proposal like ours. The chances of getting any business are very slim.

The responses indicate the different perceptions of each entity. This relates to the conscious experiential learning from similar past situations. In this case the situation being 'client meetings' or client interactions.

Moving from transactional to tactical to strategic capability requires conscious experiential knowledge acquisition.

## Moving to Higher Levels of Success

A Brain Trust (BT) is used by design or default by senior executives to achieve desirable results. However, to achieve a higher level of success an Enhanced Brain Trust (EBT) model is recommended. A few models to enhance success are outlined below. They are:

- **The Brain Trust:** The term Brain trust was coined in the 1930's for a group of close advisers to a political candidate or incumbent. These advisors, often academicians were prized for their expertise in particular fields. The inputs from these advisors were used to frame policies and to generate ideas. (Reference: Roosevelts 'Brain Trust' https://en.wikipedia.org/wiki/Brain_trust#Roosevelt's_%22Brain_Trust%22)

- **Corporate Boards:** A Board of Directors is formed to take on many responsibilities. However, their primary responsibility is to protect the shareholders' assets and ensure they receive a decent return on their investment. This sometimes can lead to excessive caution and curtailing of creativity in order to ensure ROI commitments.

- **Corporate Advisors:** These are competent consultants who advise CEO's and other senior executives on how to work towards achieving their goals. Consultants are mostly chosen for their track record and experience in specific fields. They contribute towards finding solutions to complex problems in specific areas which in turn aids in achieving overall success.

- **The Enhanced Brain Trust (EBT):** An EBT would normally consist of academicians, consultants and advisors who have an insight. Advisors are people who have conscious experiential learnings. To appreciate their contribution, it is important to understand the difference between knowledge, wisdom and insight. Academicians bring in subject knowledge. Consultants often bring in wisdom gained through experience in specific fields or business lines. The most important are advisors with insight. Insight comes from conscious situational learning. They are those who have been there and done that. They are the ones who are capable of intertwining the inputs of the other two types of advisors (academicians and consultants) and can say what will work and what will not. In a sense they provide integrated situational advice.

Finally, it must always be remembered that whatever advice is received may not cover all bases as often minute details could have been overlooked or misinterpreted. Hence it must always be kept in mind that the use of advice as it is, or in an adapted form, is your prerogative. Also, while taking important decisions you may even like to verify advice received from a second expert. The final decision is your responsibility. The skill of when and how to use advice comes from your own continuous conscious self-learning.

## Conscious Situational Self-Learning

Conscious situational learning comes from meeting the challenges and constraints of the situation being handled while executing your role. Secondly interaction with the EBT provides multi-dimensional perspectives to enhance this learning experience.

The topics discussed in the book cover areas that are not commonly considered for personal development. At higher levels 'Self-Development' is a personal responsibility. Hence personal development in such areas may require the help of coaches and mentors. To recap, the topics are: (1) Managing the Transition Journey; (2) Managing Contribution Perceptions; (3) Managing the Eco-System; (4) Managing Partnership Priorities; (5) Personal Networking; and (6) Managing Intra-Organizational and Cross-Border Conflicts.

The formation and use of an EBT will definitely enhance personal capability and at the same time help provide solutions to meet short, medium and long-term goals. Also engagement with experts in a well-managed EBT will ensure personal capability enhancement in line with the times. The learning comes from understanding the basis on which advice is given on how to achieve goals.

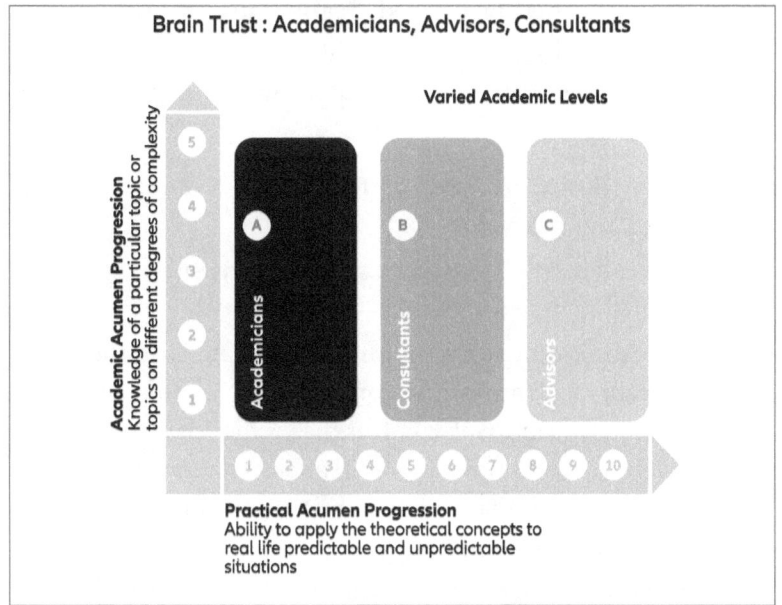

# The Way Forward

## Knowing what you know and do not know

Inherent talent brings successful top executives to their current positions. While many may know what has made them successful, it has been observed that quite a few are unaware of the nuances that led them to success. That is, they did not know what they knew and therefore could not develop themselves to higher levels. In other words, they were constrained to reach their full potential. As an example, we see several leading sports persons who were unaware of their talent potential until they were spotted by a coach. These very persons often changed coaches when migrating to higher levels of performance.

## Understanding the "Enhanced Brain Trust" model

The EBT is a tool to assist successful executives to better their performance. The three points to appreciate in using the EBT model are:

- Advisors selected are based on need and also the chemistry of the giver and receiver.
- Advisor roles will always remain informal and is not to be considered as a paid service.
- The advisor-executive relationship is based on 'Give and Take'. This means needs are satisfied on both sides without any direct monetary element involved. This makes the relationship more complex. Relationships with 'academicians and consultants' are generally more simple and straightforward in nature.

It is therefore important to learn and appreciate the EBT process. The four stages in an advisory relationship are; identification, selection, maintenance and disengagement. Each step has to be taken seriously and managed carefully to optimize returns.

## Applying and Monitoring Personal Progress

This is most important and difficult, because the EBT model is personal and private. It is not meant to be discussed or shared with others. If knowledge of an advisory circle becomes public it could lead to numerous complications, in addition to loss of personal credibility. However, if managed well there are good chances of the EBT user becoming a powerful advisor in future.

Finally, it is important to understand that at any level it is possible to have an EBT. The earlier it is started the more useful it becomes at the top. Experience has shown that many of those who had adopted the EBT model when three levels below the CEO, became very successful CEOs over time.

## One Last Word

*Many of the main topics in this book are outlined briefly. However, there are quite a few related aspects that have not been elaborated. These need to be reflected upon and if required guidance may be sought.*

*There are many areas outlined in this book that can be studied more in depth. I hope that this book motivates you to research the subject further.*

*This book and all other readings will not help you if you do not act. Remember that it is what you do that finally brings you success not what you know or what you say.*

### Remember
Self-Development is a personal responsibility
A well-managed EBT is the route to success

# Enhanced Brain Trust in a Nutshell

## Personal Advisory Connects

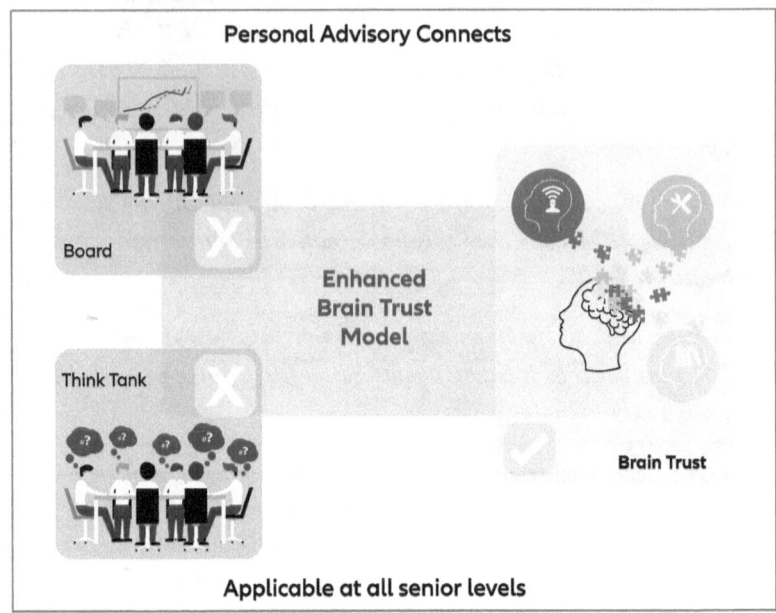

Board

Think Tank

Enhanced
Brain Trust
Model

Brain Trust

**Applicable at all senior levels**

## Personal Advisory Connects
## EBT-A combination of Experts

**Academicians :** Experts with theoretical knowledge in a specific subject.**Knowledge**

**Consultants :** Experts with experimental knowledge in a specific domain.**Wisdom**

**Advisors :** Experts with experimental integrated knowledge of multiple domains.**Insight**

**Multiple Domains:** Business, Technical, Legal, Finance, etc

## Personal Advisory Connects
## EBT - General Operating Structure

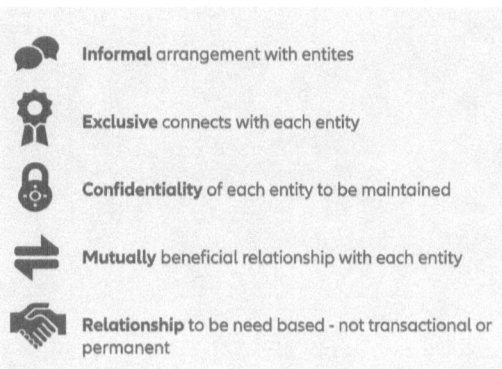

**Informal** arrangement with entites

**Exclusive** connects with each entity

**Confidentiality** of each entity to be maintained

**Mutually** beneficial relationship with each entity

**Relationship** to be need based - not transactional or permanent

## Personal Advisory Connects EBT Process

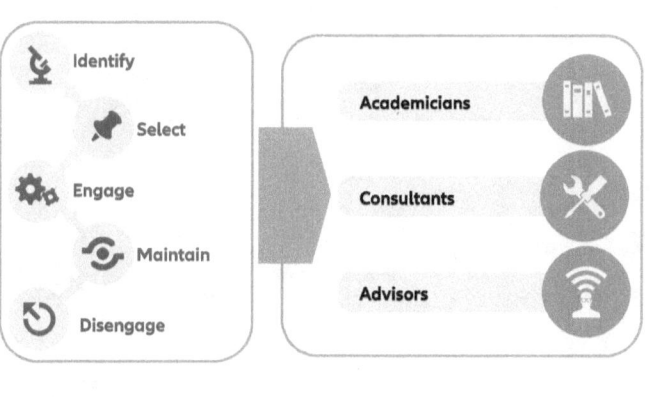

Identify

Select

Engage

Maintain

Disengage

Academicians

Consultants

Advisors

www.ingramcontent.com/pod-product-compliance
Lightning Source LLC
Chambersburg PA
CBHW030523260626
47157CB00005B/1854